So Young to Burn

By the same author in Pan Books

HOLIDAY FOR INSPECTOR WEST
MURDER, LONDON—AUSTRALIA
MURDER ON THE LINE
THE CASE OF THE INNOCENT VICTIMS
TWO FOR INSPECTOR WEST
THE SCENE OF THE CRIME
ACCIDENT FOR INSPECTOR WEST

JOHN CREASEY

So Young to Burn

UNABRIDGED

PAN BOOKS LTD : LONDON

First published 1968 by Hodder and Stoughton Ltd.
This edition published 1970 by Pan Books Ltd,
33 Tothill Street, London, S.W.1.

330 02496 5

*The characters in this book are entirely imaginary
and bear no relation to any living person*

*This book is for Lyn,
who works with such selfless
dedication at the task
of making each new book of
mine as good as it can be*
JOHN CREASEY

*Printed in Great Britain by
Richard Clay (The Chaucer Press), Ltd., Bungay, Suffolk*

Contents

CHAPTER ONE

THE YOUNG LOVERS

'LISTEN, Tony!'

'There's nothing.'

'Listen!'

'I tell you—'

'*Please listen,*' Helena Young said pleadingly. '*Please.*'

Tony Wainwright said: 'All right,' and he let the whole weight of his body fall on her, half-teasing, half-longing, impatient with desire yet knowing how sensitive she was.

Out here, on Wimbledon Common, the rustling of a summer night filled the air and crept among the bushes of hawthorn and bramble, among the heavy foliage of oak and beech and birch. Above, a star-strewn sky was pale, with a half-moon. Beyond this little clearing in the bushes were the distant lights of moving cars on the road towards Putney and Roehampton. Closer were parked cars, each with its own secrets. Not far off, a man whistled to a dog; there were no nearer sounds.

Helena said, nervously: 'I could have sworn I heard something.'

'You're imagining things.'

'I would hate—' She paused.

'What would you hate?' He eased himself up on to his elbows, but their faces were close and their bodies still touched.

'A – a Peeping Tom.'

'I'd soon fix *him.*'

'You – you don't understand,' Helena said. 'The very possibility of anyone seeing us—'

'It's dark, sweetheart.'

'Or even hearing—'

Tony lowered his head and brushed her lips with his, drew back and said very softly:

'It's all right, my darling. We won't tonight. You're – so edgy.'

'I'm sorry, darling.'

7

'You don't have to be sorry. But it won't be long now. Soon we'll have our own flat. Just imagine the curtains drawn, the world shut out!'

'It will be – wonderful!'

'*Wonderful*,' Tony echoed huskily and, he hoped, convincingly.

He knew that he should get up now, should overcome desire; that if he stayed, and wooed and won her – as he knew he could – he would have gained nothing and she would have lost a little of her trust in him. But it wasn't easy. She was so very – near. So much his. And their bodies still touched. Until that moment of imagined sound he had thought that the ecstasy of love-making was theirs to share. He wished he had not given way to her reluctance in that weak moment; he wished one did not have to promise a girl so much. Why couldn't she just *enjoy* the moments of love?

He shifted himself to one side.

'Up we get! We—'

As he moved, a blinding light flashed, once, twice, thrice, someone laughed, someone swore, and as Tony flung himself forward again, in an attempt to hide the girl, he felt tingling pains on his arms, his legs, the back of his head; and as he cried out, Helena screamed in mingled fear and pain.

Two, three, or four, perhaps five or six dark figures ran off.

Tony heaved himself to his feet, hoisted the girl over his shoulder, and running, stumbling, towards a pond close by, plunged into it. As she went under, Helena screamed and screamed again, but he kept dowsing her face and soaking himself until a small crowd of people came running to see what was the matter.

Not very far away, in Chelsea, the public houses and the picture palaces emptied, the lights were turned off, the gates and the doors locked. Families made their way home, noisily; couples went off together quietly; the lonely men and women on their own, too shy or too afraid to find a companion, returned to the myriad tiny rooms, the flatlets, the bed-sits, the small hotels, and boarding houses. Front doors, landing doors, passage doors, closed on most. The couples lingered, walking arm in arm or very close together along the dimmed streets, pausing where the shadows were darkest to kiss with a passion which betrayed their longing. In one narrow street not far from the river a couple strolled, the girl's fair head on the boy's square shoulder, step in step, happy.

They paused at a house in a terrace of white-painted houses.

'Here we are, darling,' he said.

'Like to walk to the corner and back?'

'I'd like to—' The man broke off with a short laugh. 'Come on, then.'

They walked, still touching each other.

'Jill.'

'Yes, darling.'

'I *am* a male, you know.'

'I know.'

'And this *is* the second half of the twentieth century.'

'I know that, too!'

'Then why *do* you insist on living in the nineteenth century?'

Jill said, very softly, very firmly: 'I must be an old-fashioned girl.'

'Oh, *that* old stuff. You know you'll be alone in the flat tonight – as Daisy's away.'

'Yes,' said Jill. 'I will be. Clive—'

'Yes?'

'Clive, I love you very, *very* much.'

'I love you, desperately, passionately—'

'As you have often loved before.'

'But this is different! I swear it's different!'

'If I really believed it was, then who knows how modern I might become?' They reached the corner, and turned round, like one body. 'But I don't really, darling.'

'What can I do to make you believe me?'

'To tell you the truth, I don't know,' Jill answered quite soberly. 'I simply don't know. But we mustn't argue about it any more or we'll spoil the evening.'

'You wouldn't suspect that mine *was* spoiled already, would you?'

'I hope it isn't,' Jill said, as they stopped outside her house. 'I'm sorry, darling, I—' She broke off, head jerking up. 'What's that?'

'What?' demanded Clive sulkily.

'That noise.'

'I didn't hear any noise.'

'It was at the front door.'

'Must have been your Puritan conscience.'

'No, seriously, there *was* a sound.'

'But Daisy's away.'

'Yes – that's what scares me.'

'*Scares* you!' Clive gave a contented little laugh and strode towards the door. 'Let me be Sir Galahad and—'

Before he reached it, the door burst open and four youths came rushing out, two of them leaping at him and spraying him with a liquid which fell as soft as rain, some on his face, some on his clothes and hands; in wild fury he attacked the men and sent two flying, while crying out to Jill: 'Get your clothes off, get them off!' The youths all turned and ran, while Clive Davidson rushed Jill indoors, pulling at her clothes, jumper, skirt, slip, as if he were a madman.

'If you got any on your face go and wash it, wash it off!' He pushed her towards the kitchen and then sprang to a garden hose, turned the tap full on, drenching himself from head to foot.

The church social in Shepherd's Bush had gone on much later than usual, and even when it was over the bare hall with its yellow-varnished rafters and the religious prints, the certificates of merit for the Band of Hope, notices relating to the Mothers' Union and the Boy Scouts, displayed lists of Sunday School examinations and a dozen other church affairs, was not emptied at once. Little groups stood about, holding desultory conversations, the washing-up volunteers lingered over their clattering cups and saucers; on this warm evening no one was in a hurry.

Among a dozen people of mixed ages in one corner of the hall was Betty Smith. One of seven youths in another corner was Jonathan Cobden. All the evening Betty had noticed Jonathan, who was tall, dark, pleasant-looking, glancing towards her. She was a visitor, knowing no one but the uncle and aunt and their children with whom she was staying. She saw the crowd of youths move towards the door, and the one who had attracted her attention hung back, and then came straight towards her, She flushed a deep pink, unaware that her aunt noticed it with amusement.

'I say,' Jonathan Cobden said, 'aren't you new here?'

'I'm just visiting, that's all.'

'Oh. With the Smiths?'

'Yes. Do you know them?'

'Well, yes, I – that is, they're neighbours. I – would you – I, er – would you – ah – may I walk home with you?'

Betty's eyes lit up.

'I'd love you to, if—'

They turned and looked at Betty's aunt, who had missed nothing, and who had a soft spot for young Jonathan Cobden.

'Auntie, can I—?'

'Mrs Smith, can I take Betty home?'

'Provided you take good care of her, you may.' There was a roguish gleam in Mrs Smith's eyes.

'Oh, I will!'

The older people in the group watched them walk off together and a man said wistfully:

'I wish there were more young people like that, these days.'

Betty and Jonathan were oblivious of their elders, of the other young people grinning and teasing, of everything and everyone except themselves. They walked for five minutes beneath the bright lights of Shepherd's Bush Road and then along a side street, which was not well lit. Here, their hands touched and clasped. It was for each of them the first romance; for each the first awareness of the fast beating heart, the electric thrill which seemed to come from the touch of another's fingers. Neither of them spoke; neither needed to speak, until at the end of this street Jonathan said:

'Now we're nearly there.'

'Yes. Just across the road.'

'Would it – would it be all right if we walked round again?'

'I – I should think so.'

'I'd *love* to,' Jonathan said, adding with sudden boldness: 'I think you're *won*derful! I've never seen a girl like you before.'

Betty's tongue seemed to cleave to the roof of her mouth as she tried to say 'Haven't you?' She couldn't get the words out and the very effort made her tighten her grip and seemed to draw Jonathan towards her. Without a word they were in each other's arms, kissing.

11

As they stood there in their fleeting innocence, three youths came racing along the street towards them, the clatter of footsteps startling and alarming. The youths, only a few yards away, began to whoop and leap up and down, prancing about the couple wildly, flinging out an arm, snatching at Betty's long hair, pulling out Jonathan's tie, spanking her bottom, slapping his face, spinning them round and round until they were giddy as well as terrified, breathless, helpless.

Then suddenly a dark shadow fell over them, and a man said in a deep, calm voice:

'That's enough.'

Two of the youths turned and raced away, the other was gripped by a policeman who had just turned the corner. For a split second everything was quite still, the only sounds the thudding footsteps of the running youths, the gasping of Betty and Jonathan. Then the captured youth kicked out savagely at the policeman. The kick caught him agonizingly on the ankle and he cried out and released his grip. The youth turned to run after his mates.

Jonathan Cobden had just straightened up. He saw what happened, saw the policeman reel away, and almost without thinking he launched himself bodily at the youth.

'*Don't!*' screamed Betty.

She need not have worried. Taken completely unawares, the youth was struck by the full force of Jonathan's rush, staggered back several yards, then tripped and fell. He banged the back of his head on the pavement with such a thud that it sounded above all other sounds. When the policeman recovered and moved forward, Jonathan stood with his arm round Betty as they stared at the motionless figure. From the main road end of the street, men came running – Betty's uncle and the wistful man among them.

'Betty!'

'Are you all right?'

'What happened?'

In a clear throbbing voice, Betty said: 'He was wonderful, *wonderful.*'

For a moment everyone stopped, seemed almost to stop breathing, and looked at her. Then the policeman, small as London policemen go, and at this moment feeling acutely conscious of his own failure, spoke with feeling:

'He certainly was. Now we'd better get an ambulance – that chap looks as if he needs attention.'

At about the same time as the attack on Betty and Jonathan, two youths turned into Bell Street, Chelsea, one very tall and slender, the other shorter and much broader. He was on the kerb side; listening. They were brothers, Martin and Richard West; and as usual Richard did most of the talking.

'... all I can say is, there's far too much emphasis on what we do wrong, nothing like enough on what we do *right* ... To hear some of these old fogies talk you'd think that no one under twenty-one ever had an idea or ever accepted a responsibility. And that's rot. Absolute rot!'

'Have you?' interpolated Martin, often called Scoop.

'Have I what?'

'Ever accepted a responsibility?' Martin asked solemnly.

'You know darned well I—' Richard caught his breath, suddenly aware that he was falling into a well-laid trap, and his tone changed. '*You're* my responsibility, brother! I don't know where you'd be without me. *You* can talk!'

Martin gave a broad, attractive grin.

'So can you, if it comes to that. I—'

They broke off, for as they neared their home the front door opened and their father, Chief Superintendent Roger West of New Scotland Yard, came hurrying out. He caught sight of them, waved, and said:

'Get the car out for me, Fish – I'll be there in a minute.' He dived back into the house, while Richard-called-Fish stepped to the garage and Martin hooked back the double gates near the road. The black Rover car was at the kerbside, the engine ticking over, when Roger West appeared again, massive and quick moving, as if he could not get where he wanted to go fast enough.

'Big job, Pop?' asked Martin.

'Don't know yet,' said Roger West, and as Richard climbed out of his car, he went on: 'London youth on the rampage again. I hope you two soon grow up.'

'*Well!*' gasped Richard, and glared as his father took the wheel.

CHAPTER TWO

CHIEF SUPERINTENDENT ROGER WEST

ROGER WEST heard his younger son's 'Well!' and guessing what caused it grinned at him, and winked at Martin as he drove off. He went too fast, but slowed down at the approach to the corner of this pleasant Chelsea Street which led into Kings Road on the one hand and, by devious ways, to the Embankment on the other. It was nearly eleven o'clock, and most of the homecoming traffic from London's West End and theatreland had passed, but there was still a steady stream of traffic coming out of town. He turned towards the West End, passing the little shops, every other one of which had paintings or antiques spotlighted in the window. Here and there he passed couples, arms linked, bodies close, oblivious of everything but each other. In a dark shop doorway a man and a girl were quarrelling, the girl's face bitter with anger. Young love! Roger gave a wry, uneasy smile, for 'young love' had suffered a great deal tonight, according to the report which had called him from his home, his long-suffering wife, and a television documentary on 'Student Violence Round the World'.

Student violence – teenage viciousness – juvenile delinquency – it did not matter under what name it was headlined, the growing problem was a real and menacing one to the authorities and, in one way or another, to the police. Roger was uneasily aware, as were many officials at Scotland Yard, that it was getting out of hand. The phrase passed through his mind, and as he rounded Sloane Square and headed for Buckingham Palace and Birdcage Walk, he took himself to task. 'It was getting out of hand.' What was 'it'? A few hundred, possibly a few thousand young people from a cross-section of society were reacting violently against society, some of them with inborn criminal tendencies, some taking the law into their own hands, others carried away by the excitement, the thrill of rebelling against the law. The motivation was not all-important to a policeman, who had to deal with effects, not causes, but if one could find the motivation one was often halfway towards prevention, and that meant halfway towards a cure.

He turned into Birdcage Walk; on either side, lingering in the shadows, were many young lovers – as there were in all of London's parks.

He drove along the north side of Parliament Square, past the floodlit Houses of Parliament and the huge moon-face of Big Ben. It began to strike the quarter as he turned off the Embankment and into the Yard. He parked close to the steps and hurried up them, acknowledged by several policemen on duty and two detectives, all obviously preoccupied. The Yard was always dead by night except in the Information Room. He turned into his own office, which overlooked the Embankment, and out of its darkness he saw the lights of Westminster Bridge, of the new Shell House, and of the Festival Hall shimmering on the dark, oily-looking surface of the Thames. He switched on a light and picked up the internal telephone, dialled Information and, when a man answered, said:

'West. What's new?'

'About the Wimbledon Common job?'

'Yes.'

'The man's in a nasty way, in hospital. Name of Wainwright.'

'The girl?'

'I'm not—' there was a pause, and voices sounded away from the telephone. 'You there, sir?'

Where was he expected to be?

'Yes.'

'Mr Ibbottson of Chelsea is on his way as you requested, sir, and so is Mr Moriarty of Wimbledon. They will have the latest information.'

'What about the Shepherd's Bush incident?'

'No harm done there, sir, and the prisoner is on his way to Cannon Row – should arrive in ten minutes or so, sir.'

'Who's with him?'

'I'm not sure, sir.'

'Well, make sure, and see that I'm told when I reach Cannon Row.'

'Yes, sir.'

'And if Mr Ibbottson or Mr Moriarty arrive before I look in to see you, ask them to come and wait in my office.'

'Very good, sir.'

Roger rang off, scowled at the window, wondered whether

15

he was in a worse mood than he need be, and stared into the night. The crop of crimes being committed both by the young and against the young was getting under his skin. There were so many and it was difficult to distinguish the serious ones from those that were little more than pranks. These days, a prank could develop alarmingly into something more serious. Whether one liked to admit it or not, there *was* a wave of brutality in London, one that could easily get out of hand unless it were kept in check. His job was to keep it in check.

After ten minutes or so he went out, gave instructions about the two Divisional men in the main hall, went down the steps and across to the entrance to Cannon Row Police Station, which was adjacent to but not part of the Yard. A man approached from the doorway.

'Mr King – Chief Inspector King – is here with the prisoner from Shepherd's Bush, sir.'

'Thanks.' The advance information gave Roger a few seconds to adjust himself to the character of the officer he was going to see. He knew King, one of the older, more reliable but less adventurous men on the Metropolitan Force, a family man with a Methodist background.

King, thin, with a slight stoop and a rather droll expression, was waiting for him in the charge-room.

'Hallo, King. Sorry to drag you out,' Roger said.

'I thought I'd dragged *you* out,' King replied. 'Ours wasn't the only job tonight, I gather.'

'Two others reported so far,' Roger told him. 'This chap you've picked up might give us a lead.'

'I shouldn't think so,' said King. 'I doubt if he's in a gang, just one of the young devils who get out of control. If it weren't for the general situation, though, I'd have charged him locally. As a matter of fact we nearly lost him. The kid who was attacked...' He told the story briefly, letting Roger reflect on the honesty of the constable who had made the arrest as well as the courage of the boy. 'According to relatives, this couple were only walking home together.'

'Has the prisoner talked?'

'Won't open his mouth, sir.'

'Anything found on him?'

'Just his name and address, and he's not on our records.'

'Where's he from?'

16

'Camberwell,' King answered.

'Hmm,' said Roger. 'Not a local lout, then.' He moved about restlessly, frowning. 'I was going to talk to him myself, but that could make him feel too important. I'm not sure—' he hesitated, before going on : 'I'm not sure it wouldn't be best to take him back and have him charged in the morning with run-of-the-mill common assault. That will warn some of the young louts off. The Press won't take much notice of it, but they certainly would if we charged him here.' He paused, and then asked : 'Any ideas yourself?'

'I think you're right,' said King.

'Had much trouble with youngsters down your way?'

'Not much more than usual,' King answered. 'We've always had our share. Can't understand what gets into the kids, nowadays. Life's too easy for them, I suppose.'

'Could be,' said Roger. If that was what King thought he was not likely to shift in his opinion; youth was already condemned. 'You've seen my general request, haven't you?'

'Yes.' King drew a folded sheet of paper out of his pocket. 'I was reading it again on the way up, sir. Really going to town on the young brutes at last.'

Brutes.

'Yes,' Roger said. 'And I'm landed with the job.'

'Can't imagine anyone who would be better, Super.'

'Thanks,' said Roger drily. 'I can imagine a lot of jobs I'd like more. Do you suspect any personal reason for the attack on this pair – what are their names, by the way?'

'Jonathan Cobden and Betty Smith. No, absolutely none at all. The boy's from a good, church-going family, only sixteen, rather young for his age, and the girl's visiting relations – she's from Reading. No doubt about it, that was just a chance attack by three young hooligans – young sadists, if you ask me.'

'Yes.'

'You know what I think, sir?'

Roger guessed : You think we ought to bring back the birch. Aloud, he asked : 'What do you think?'

'Flogging's too good for these young brutes.'

'Could be,' Roger said non-committally. 'I'll have someone spend ten minutes with your prisoner, and get you to charge him at West London Court in the morning.'

'Right!' King straightened up. 'And I'll see you get all the help we can give you.' He tapped the fold of paper. 'Had any luck yet?'

'It's only been out two days,' Roger reminded him.

He left Cannon Row a few minutes later, dissatisfied with himself, with King, with the situation; and as he walked through the pleasant night air to the Yard, he tried to laugh at himself. Two squad cars roared and raced out of the courtyard to answer some urgent summons, perhaps a report of another attack on another couple. Returning to his office, he pictured the memorandum which King had taken out of his pocket. Two men were standing with their backs to the door, reading a copy of the same memo, which was pinned to a small bulletin board on the wall.

The men spun round.

Chief Inspector Moriarty of Wimbledon was the shorter, a compact, well-dressed handsome man with close-cropped dark hair and a a jowl blue from incipient stubble. There was at once the look of an Irishman and an American about him, the faintest trace of Irish brogue in his pleasant voice, of Irish heritage in his blue, deep-set eyes.

'Good evening, Superintendent.'

'Hallo,' said Roger, shaking hands.

Ibbottson of Chelsea was a bigger, broader, heavier man with a pale face and a double chin. His Lancashire brogue was unmistakable.

'Glad to meet you again, Mr West.'

'And you,' Roger said. 'Sit down.' As he went behind his desk, they pulled up chairs. He himself was in the middle-forties, his fair hair hiding the grey. He was good-looking enough to have once earned the nickname 'Handsome', which, over the years, had stuck. He was still the youngest Chief Superintendent at the Yard and couldn't get much higher. His position and the improbability of early promotion gave him a sense of stability, a confidence in himself which made itself felt. Sitting there, he was like the chairman at a committee meeting.

'What I need to find out, is whether there *is* a pattern in these attacks on young couples, and whether the different kinds of juvenile and teenage crimes are in any way connected. The only way to find out, as far as I can see, is to get the opinion of the Divisions first – then try to analyse the opinions – or the conclusions – of the Divisions. As the memo says I don't think it's going to be much use going back over the old crimes – we want to make a clean start.'

Moriarty was watching him very attentively. Ibbottson pursed his full lips, and nodded.

'So we want all possible detail about tonight's attacks.' Roger said, 'and when we've got it, we want to compare the cases phase by phase. I've asked all Divisions to put the inquiry into the hands of one officer – but you know that.'

'Tell you what *I* think,' said Ibbottson.

'Glad to hear it.'

'There always *have* been some bad ones among the young and they aren't much worse today than they were in *my* young days. There's a danger of making too much fuss over what they do, by giving them a false sense of their own importance. And if you ask me, the couple in my manor asked for trouble. My God, the things the long-haired idiots get up to in Chelsea!'

Roger thought: He doesn't want to be bothered.

'Take the young fellow in my manor,' Ibbottson went on. 'When my chap got there, he'd cut and run. She might have been raped a dozen times for all *he* cared. You can't do anything with slobs like that except smack 'em down hard when you get the chance. *He* wasn't much better than the assailants.'

'How did this couple ask for trouble?' asked Roger.

'Necking, if that's the word, on the street.'

Roger said: 'The girl was practically naked and in hysteria when she was found, wasn't she? And her clothes had been sprayed with what we think was sulphuric acid – the fabric just tore apart.'

'Yes. Lucky for her her face wasn't touched,' Ibbottson said.

'Lucky for her that her boy-friend had the presence of mind to tear her clothes off, or she would have had some nasty body burns,' Roger said gruffly.

'Anyway, after that one selfless deed, the boy-friend didn't stay with her,' Ibbottson said drily. 'It's my contention that provided no one's seriously injured, a bit of rough stuff might make the streets a bit more respectable.' Hastily he added: 'I'm speaking off the record, mind you.'

'So I gathered,' Roger said. He could not recall feeling so hostile towards a senior policeman for a long time.

'I'll catch the baskets, if I can,' Ibbottson began.

'But if you don't, the local girls are likely to be more discreet in future – is that it?'

'I'll bet they will! This particular girl's under sedation, and I've a woman officer sitting in her room to take a statement when she comes round.'

'Have the special instructions been spread round in your Division?' Roger asked.

'Aye, the Superintendent didn't lose a minute,' Ibbottson replied. 'All crimes committed by, or on, young people are to be reported immediately to Division and by Division to you. And each one will have one of your forms, Mr West.'

Roger said: 'Right, thanks.' He felt tired and depressed, for Ibbottson so obviously thought he was making too much fuss. Ibbottson looked tired, too, and old; perhaps he was past it.

'Will you let me have a written report tomorrow?' He stood up, and Ibbottson rose and stepped towards the door. 'Good-night.' The door opened and closed, and Ibbottson's footsteps sounded heavy in the passage for a few moments, but soon faded.

Roger turned to Moriarty. 'Your man didn't manage to run away, I gather.'

'My man's got third-degree burns from acid all over his backside, his legs, and the back of his head,' Moriarty answered, 'and the girl's got burns on her forehead and on one cheek. If the man hadn't protected her with his body and dashed off to the Leg o' Mutton Pond they'd have been much worse. I can imagine Peeping Toms taking photographs for the hell of it, or for blackmail, but when it comes to throwing acid – that was done for a purpose.' Moriarty paused, as if wondering whether he was saying too much, but then went on: 'That's my opinion, sir.'

CHAPTER THREE

MOTIVES?

MORIARTY SAT square and tense, obviously prepared for dis-
agreement, even disapproval. His eyes were so deeply
shadowed he might have been wearing artificial lashes. His
intensity was clear in the way he gripped his hands, one on his
knee, one on the wooden arm of his chair.

'A purpose doesn't get us far,' Roger said. 'What purpose?'

'If we know there is one it should put us on the right
track.'

'This particular purpose could have been for the pleasure of
inflicting pain. Is that what you mean?'

'No, sir, I don't think that's it. A sadist would want to see
his victims suffer, wouldn't be satisfied to spray them and run
off. And it was dark – they couldn't even be sure they had
caused pain.'

This man had a lively intelligence.

'If not sadism – what?' asked Roger.

'There are two possibilities,' Moriarty stated flatly.

'*Only* two?'

'Only two that I've thought of.'

'That's better.'

Moriarty frowned – and then relaxed into a flashing smile
which made him look nearer his age; he was in the middle-
thirties, but in moods of tension might have been ten years
older.

'It could have been a personal attack on this couple, or the
man,' he said. 'From a jealous lover, a husband, even a
brother.' Roger made no comment. 'Or could have been a kind
of warning.'

'Warning to whom?'

Moriarty said: 'Young lovers on Wimbledon Common.' He
spoke the words very carefully, obviously half-prepared to be
derided. Roger saw how his knuckles blanched, how the lines
compressed at the corner of his eyes and lips. These gradually
smoothed out, and they vanished completely when Roger
said:

'A kind of clean-up campaign?'

'*You've* thought of that, sir?'

Roger said drily: 'Yes, I've thought of it, but as I see it, there are at least two other possible causes – one of them not truly a motive. It could be a crop of imitative crimes, a mixture of prurience and sexual frustration or even perversion. And it could be the act of a man who's not right in the head.'

'Yes – I suppose so, but – *imitative*?'

Roger said quietly: 'We've had five cases of acid throwing in the parks and commons in London in the past four weeks.'

'I know,' Moriarty conceded. 'Epping Forest, Hampstead Heath, Regent's Park, Hyde Park, and now Wimbledon Common. Do you seriously think these *are* imitative crimes?'

'I think they could be.'

'I was working on the assumption that they were all done by the same crowd,' Moriarty told him. 'The acid used was the same in each case – concentrated sulphuric.'

Roger asked sharply: 'How do you know?'

'I checked with each Division, sir.'

'So you've been working on this, have you?'

'Take it from me, I have.'

Roger said: 'Why? Haven't you got plenty of work on your plate?'

'More than enough,' agreed Moriarty. 'It's hard to say just why, sir, except that when I joined the Force, twelve years ago, the first case I worked on was one of acid throwing. A young girl in the neighbourhood had turned down one man for another, and the jilted one threw concentrated sulphuric acid on her. It was—'

'The Parradise case?' Roger interrupted.

'Yes, sir. You were in charge – it was the first time I'd ever seen you. I found the girl in a back yard, moaning. I was badly shaken – never really got over it, I suppose. For my money, it's the worst crime in the calendar.'

'There aren't many worse,' Roger admitted thoughtfully. 'So you think the same people do all of this acid throwing. What makes you regard that as a possibility?'

'Every case has basic similarities,' answered Moriarty. 'A spot where couples often get together is chosen. There's no warning to speak of – this girl thought she heard a sneeze but wasn't sure. There are flashlights, and presumably photographs—'

'Only presumably?'

'They could let the flashes off to dazzle the victims and see what they're doing,' reasoned Moriarty. 'After the flashes comes the acid. This is the first time the man in the case has thrown himself back over the girl. The natural impulse when there's a flash is to jump off – which means the girl usually gets the worst of the acid – which is always sprayed.'

'From a spray gun?'

'A spray of some sort,' said Moriarty. 'Er – this shows what I mean, sir.' He took out a folded sheet of paper, and smoothed it out in front of Roger. In the middle were rough outlines of two bodies, close together, and round the bodies were roughly drawn circles. These circles were of five different colours – black, green, red, blue, and purple. They did not coincide exactly, but were all about the same circumference. 'Here's a diagram of the area of the acid-fall – in each case the grass and bushes were closely examined for acid burns and the radius was drawn; I've seen each one and copied them on top of one another. Tonight's is the purple ring. See what that means?' asked Moriarty eagerly.

Roger nodded but did not interrupt.

'It suggests that the same size spray from about the same height and the same force was used, and the user made sure the wind was behind him. Wouldn't you think that pointed to the same man using it?'

'It's an indication,' Roger admitted.

'So we ought to be able to find him!'

'Yes,' Roger said slowly. 'We need other things, though – the source of the acid, and the type of spray. Was anything else found? Footprints, cigarette-stubs, hair?'

'Nothing identifiable,' Moriarty said. 'Until tonight.'

'What did you get tonight?'

'A footprint in a patch of damp earth,' answered Moriarty with satisfaction. 'I've had a cast made and photographs taken. It's a size nine and a half, slightly worn at the toe and heel, and with a very even tread. What I'd like—' He broke off.

'What would you like?' encouraged Roger.

'Well, I'm speaking out of turn,' Moriarty confessed with an embarrassed laugh. 'But some of these investigations might have been a little sketchy. The first two weren't taken seriously enough – not that I'm criticizing, but some of us *are* a bit casual about a chap being caught with his pants down. No one *says*, "serve him right", but the implication's there all right.'

As it had been with Ibbottson and to a lesser degree with King.

'No difficulty about checking on what we've got,' Roger said. 'I've all the files here.'

Moriarty's eyes lit up.

'If I could stay and study them—'

'No home to go to?'

Moriarty laughed. 'I'm not married – it's easier to be a copper when you're single!'

'Stay here and look at them,' Roger invited.

'Thanks! Er – mind if I ask you one question, sir?'

'Go on.'

'Why did you send out the memorandum?'

That was a long story and not one for Moriarty yet. It was three years since Roger, investigating the murder of an old man by a gang of youths, had really started it. By chance, half a dozen or more crimes involving young people had been assigned to him; in his way he had become expert, studying the motives and minds of young criminals as well as of young people who had gone wild, fallen to temptation or been lured into crime by bad company. Being father of two sons of the age group he was investigating had made his interest close and personal. He had spent a lot of time thinking and analysing the causes, the social groups concerned, meeting not only hundreds of young people but Youth Club workers, social workers, Probation and Welfare Officers. For years this had been regarded as a social problem, the police dealing only with the effects. A week ago, however, the Home Office had asked the Commissioner of the Metropolitan Police for an official survey from the point of view of the police. Coppell, the Commander of the Criminal Investigation Department, had sent for Roger.

'It's obviously your job, West.'

'It's a full-time one, sir.'

'I know. Concentrate on it for two or three weeks, and let me know how it shapes up.' Coppell, a man of few words, had pushed his chair back in dismissal.

Now, to Moriarty, Roger said simply: 'The Powers That Be are getting worried about all aspects of juvenile crime.'

'And about time too,' Moriarty said feelingly. 'Before we know where we are the country will be run by teenagers.' He gave a forced, staccato little laugh. 'Some of them *are* getting out of hand.'

'Yes. Well, you study these files' – Roger took the four files from a wooden Pending tray on his desk – 'and then tell me if you think we can improve on this questionnaire.' He tapped the list on the wall just behind him. 'I'm going home. Call me in the morning, will you?'

Moriarty stood up.

'Be sure I will, sir!'

Roger said: 'One other thing.'

'Yes?'

'The young couple who were burned on Wimbledon Common – what about their parents?'

'The girl's an only daughter,' Moriarty said. 'She seemed as worried about the parents knowing as about the burns. The man's an Australian, who lives in London on his own. I don't know whether he has any close relatives.'

'Seen the girl's?' asked Roger.

Moriarty looked startled. 'Well, no.'

Roger said: 'Bit rough on them, isn't it?'

Moriarty said: 'It didn't occur to me.'

'Tricky situation,' Roger admitted. 'Especially for a bachelor. Where does she live, do you remember?'

'In Putney – 17a Wilderness Street.'

'Off the Thames and over the Lower Richmond Road,' Roger remarked. 'I think I'll go and look them up.' When Moriarty simply stared, he went on a little self-consciously: 'It never does any harm to have people on our side. And if we help the girl with her parents, she may talk more freely to us – may remember something she's forgotten. And remember it *could* have been done by a jealous ex-boy-friend.'

'Yes, I see what you mean.' Moriarty gave another staccato laugh. 'Certain advantages in being a family man, aren't there?'

'Well, yes,' Roger said drily. 'Advantages, too, in having dealt with sulphuric acid burns before. We know that it's likely that the two men – Wainwright and the one who ran away – realized what had happened to them before the acid began to burn, don't we?'

'Do we, sir?' Moriarty looked puzzled.

'Work out what that means for yourself,' Roger advised.

He was smiling to himself as he left the Yard. When he drove past the end of Bell Street he thought wistfully of Janet his wife, in bed and no doubt asleep, and of young Richard's outraged 'Well!' He chuckled, but soon sobered. Neither of his sons was particularly girl-conscious, so far as he knew, but how much *did* he know about what they got up to? What did Helena Young's parents know about their daughter, for instance?

And how much did Moriarty know about the effects of concentrated sulphuric acid?

Roger found Number 17a Wilderness Street, one of a terrace of narrow three-storeyed houses, without difficulty. Although it was half past twelve, a light was shining behind the fanlight of the front door, and when he reached it he heard voices. He pressed the bell, and there was immediate silence. Soon footsteps sounded, and the door was opened by a short but very broad man. His face was against the light, and it was impossible to see his features or his expression, but his voice was harsh and his manner brusque.

'Yes, what is it?'

'I'm from—' began Roger.

'If you're from the newspapers you can stop wasting my time *and* yours.'

Roger's heart dropped.

'Have the Press been here already?'

'All they want is their dirty sensation,' the man rasped. 'Who *are* you?'

'I'm from New Scotland Yard, the officer in charge of the investigation. Can you spare me a few minutes, Mr Young? You are Mr Young, aren't you?'

Slowly, the man answered: 'Yes, I'm Helena's father. That's what you really want to know, isn't it? And you want to know whether my daughter makes a habit of going out on the common with men. Well, I can tell you this – she won't ever go out on the common from *my* house again. Dear God, that such a thing should happen to *me*.'

Roger felt a hardening of dislike.

'Mr Young, I really think we should talk indoors—'

'I've told you all *I've* got to say!'

'I hope you haven't,' Roger said quietly. 'This was a very ugly crime indeed, and we intend to catch the men who committed it.'

'Not with my help, you won't,' replied Young. 'If you catch them there'll be a trial and *then* won't the newspapers have a Roman holiday! It's happened, it's a wicked disgrace, and I intend to be dissociated both from the disgusting episode and from my daughter. If you've got any influence, you can make sure she isn't sent back here from the hospital.'

Very slowly and deliberately, Roger said: 'Judging from your attitude, Mr Young, this would be the last place she would want to come, and the last place she should come. No wonder she's terrified of the thought of you finding out.'

'She should have considered that before!'

'*Albert!*' a woman called from along the passage, and a shadow appeared, soon the figure of a woman, a small, slight woman whose hair was a frizzy mop against the light behind her. 'You're to stop talking like this at once! You know very well you're as anxious as anyone to help her.'

The way she spoke told Roger that she must have keyed herself up to say all this. Her voice quivered and between sentences she took in deep, shuddery breaths. As she drew nearer, she put up her hands defensively, as if she half expected her husband to turn on her.

Roger said: 'Thanks to her companion, she isn't badly hurt. But *he* is.'

'If he dies it will only be what he deserves,' Young said raspingly. 'I never did like the man, I never trusted him' – he turned to his wife – 'if you'd had *your* way they would have the freedom of my front room.'

'If they had, this wouldn't have happened!' cried Mrs Young.

Young struck out at her, and Roger grabbed his arm. At that very instant a vivid flash lit up the doorway and the street close by. There was a sharp click, as of a camera, then a clatter of footsteps as a man turned and raced towards the river end of the street.

CHAPTER FOUR

FLASHLIGHT PHOTOGRAPHS

ROGER HEARD the woman cry out, the man gasp, the footsteps thud. He spun round and raced after the photographer, a man of medium height who was running very fast, a dark silhouette against a street lamp. Roger dug his elbow into his side and followed with furious speed.

Too late, he saw a figure emerge from a doorway on his right.

Too late, he saw the newcomer thrust out a leg.

He tried to jump clear, missed, and pitched forward. He had just enough warning to turn his left shoulder to the ground as he crashed down. The jolt went through his body, jarring his teeth. He lay there, helpless, taking in a deep breath against the pain, fearful of kicks or blows which might come.

None did.

He heard the stuttering noise of a motor-cycle engine, but although he raised his head, he could see only a blur of light. Slowly, he got to his feet. The stuttering noise faded, the only sound remaining being the blood throbbing in his ears as his heart thumped. He leaned against a gate post, moistened his lips, and then heard footsteps behind him.

'Are you all right?' It was Albert Young.

'I – soon will be.'

'Did they hurt you?'

'Tripped me up, yes.'

'You should have caught them.'

'Yes.'

'Now they've photographed *me*,' Young said bitterly. 'That picture will be in all the papers, too, you mark my words.'

Could that have been the Press? Roger asked himself. No, he decided, no newspaperman would go to those lengths to get a picture. He didn't disabuse Young; he was in no state or mood for an argument, yet one seemed unavoidable. 'I still want to ask those questions, Mr Young.'

Young said adamantly: 'I'm not answering any questions, and you can tell my daughter she needn't come back ever. That's *final*.'

28

He turned on his heel and stalked away.

Roger sat at the wheel of his car for a few minutes, his head aching badly, stiffness and discomfort developing in his left shoulder. If he had any sense he would go to the Yard and get a work-out; if he went straight home to bed he would probably have difficulty in moving his shoulder tomorrow. His mood was as glum as it could be. He had served no purpose except to deepen the conflict between the Youngs, and to allow that picture to be taken. And he had learned a little more about the worst side of human nature. What got into men like Young? What would get him if *he* had daughters and not sons? What did his sons get up to?

'This is plain morbid!' he exclaimed, and thrust his left arm forward to switch on the engine. Pain streaked through his shoulder. 'Wonder who's on duty at the Yard?' he asked himself. He could shake down there, avoid disturbing Janet, and go home for breakfast.

For the second time he drove rather wistfully past the end of Bell Street, and was halfway between there and the Yard when his radio-telephone began to buzz. Gingerly he unhooked the receiver.

'West.'

'Calling Superintendent West.'

'Superintendent West speaking.'

'Information Room here, sir. There is a report of another acid-throwing incident at Edmonton – in the local park, sir.'

Edmonton! In North London.

'Anyone seriously hurt?' Roger asked.

'A girl's been badly burned, sir.'

'Is Chief Inspector Moriarty still at the Yard?'

'He's standing right by me.'

'Put him on,' ordered Roger, and a moment later: 'Moriarty – go to Edmonton right away, will you? I'll square it with your Division. Call me at the Yard when you've had time to size it up.'

'Yes, sir! Think they could have had time to go from Wimbledon to Edmonton?' That question betrayed Moriarty's eagerness, his enthusiasm and unexpected lack of experience.

'Just about,' Roger said.

When he hooked the receiver on, he drove on frowning. Moriarty believed that this was the work of an organized group. If he set out to establish just that it could spoil his judgement and make it impossible for him to see the facts dispassionately. He must be watched closely. What would he have said had he been told about the photographic flash at Putney, for instance? As he drove on, Roger's mood was brighter: whether he would, or would not, go back to the Yard had been settled for him.

He had a mental glimpse of his wife's face when he had told her why he had to go out tonight; of her look of distaste.

'I wish you weren't on this assignment, Roger.'

He could have argued, but he knew it was a sore subject with her, so he had kissed her lightly on the forehead and said:

'Needs must when the devil drives!'

She hadn't been amused; and a minute later his cryptic, 'I hope you two soon grow up,' had been intended at least as much for Janet as for the boys.

He reached the Yard a little after two o'clock and went straight up to the first-aid room, where a burly sergeant was on duty. One of the beds was occupied by a man with a bandaged head.

'Had a row with a drunk,' the attendant said. 'Let's have a look at this arm, sir ... can't get it up any higher? ... Try ... Here, let me help you off with the vest ... Better?' He prodded and gripped. 'Hurt? ... Hurt? ... Hurt? ... Ah, *that's* where it is, is it? Bruised that shoulder muscle I would say, no sign of anything broken. I'll rub some liniment in, that'll help ... Don't use it too much for a day or two; I'd have a driver, if I were you ...' He had big, firm, gentle hands. 'Headache? ... Daresay it does, stiffened your neck up a bit, but I can soon fix that ... *There* you are, sir. Couple of aspirins and a snort of whisky and you'll be all right if you watch that shoulder ... Had more acid-throwing trouble, haven't you? ... I'd acid them, I'd soak their whatsits in the stuff ... Bad enough if a couple *have* to go out in the park. Ever know anyone who wouldn't prefer a bed? You know what *I* think, sir?'

'What do you think?' Roger was fascinated.

'Half of us British still think Queen Victoria's alive, that's what I think. Look at the extra work it gives *us* protecting the code of morals someone drew up a hundred years ago. Hope I'm not speaking out of turn, sir.'

Roger was thinking of Albert Young and his feeling of bitter shame.

'No,' Roger said. 'Every angle's interesting. Finished?' Gingerly he put on his vest and shirt.

'Better, sir?'

'A little easier.'

'Smell a bit like a horse doctor, but you'll soon be all right.'

'Thanks.' Roger went downstairs and to his own office. There were no messages, but on his desk, where Moriarty had sat, was one of the questionnaires which he had drawn up. On it were a number of pencilled notes in a clear, backward-sloping writing – was Moriarty left-handed?

Speeding towards North London, Moriarty was saying to himself in a curious, almost savagely restrained way :

'Now I've got a start I'll show them how to do the job. Got to give West credit for that – it didn't take him long to realize that I'm good.'

Roger, his doubts of Moriarty still on his mind, studied the questionnaire on his desk. It was headed :

CRIMINAL ACTIVITY OF YOUNG PEOPLE

Increasing incidence of crime committed by young people, between the ages of 14 and 21, may require a revision of police methods of coping, and this questionnaire is designed to obtain a comprehensive overall picture of such criminal activities in the area controlled by Metropolitan Police Force. Four specimens of Questionnaire Forms are enclosed for each Divisional HQ. One form should be filled out for each offence, and forms should be returned weekly on July 7th, 14th, 21st, and 28th. Each batch should be returned, completed, to Chief Superintendent Roger West at New Scotland Yard. Supplies of forms can be obtained on request or copied if facilities are freely available.

Date   *Time of offence   a.m.*   *Nature of Crime*

                                      p.m.

Name of suspect .... Sex ....
Age of suspect ....
Number of victims....................... Sex ....
Age of victims............................
Number of accomplices, if any.............

Number of previous offences . . . . (if none state none)
Home background of suspect . . . .
Home background of victims . . . .
Social background of suspect . . . .
Social background of victims . . . .
Educational background of suspect . . . .
Educational background of victims . . . .
Sexual reputation of suspect, if known . . . . . .
Sexual reputation of victims, if known . . . . . .
Attitude of suspect on arrest . . . .
Attitude of victims when questioned . . . .

(Moriarty had pencilled – 'Why the interest in the victims?')

Nature of Offence (Place a tick against type whenever possible, if not listed or if not precisely defined under any heading give details in space provided.)

Arson (felony) . . . .
Assault, aggravated . . . .
Assault, common . . . .
Assault, indecent . . . .
Assault on Police
  (misdemeanour) . . . .
Blackmail (felony) . . . .
Brawling (misdemeanour) . . . .
Breach of the peace
  (misdemeanour) . . . .
Bribery (misdemeanour) . . . . . .
Burglary (felony) . . . .
Careless driving . . . .
. . . .
Coin, making counterfeit (felony)
. . . .
Coin, uttering counterfeit with
  intent (misdemeanour) . . . . . .
. . . .
Confidence trick (felony) . . . . . .
Damage, wilful . . . .
Dangerous driving . . . .
Dangerous Drugs . . . .
Drunkenness . . . .
Firearms, possession . . . .
Found in enclosed premises . . . .
Gaming in Public Place
  (summary offence) . . . .
Grievous bodily harm, wounding
  with intent to cause . . . .

Housebreaking (felony) . . . .
Possessing housebreaking
  implements . . . .
Larceny – all kinds except ang-
  ling in daytime (felony . . . . . .
. . . .
Menaces, demanding money with
. . . .
Murder (felony) . . . .
Murder, conspiracy to (mis-
  demeanour) . . . .
Obstructing Police (summary
  offence) . . . .
Rape (felony) . . . .
Receiving stolen property . . . . . .
Resisting stolen property . . . . . .
Resisting Police . . . .
Robbery (felony) . . . .
Taking away motor vehicle . . . .
Causing Wilful damage . . . .
Wounding, unlawful (mis-
  demeanour) . . . .
Wounding with intent to maim,
  etc. (felony) . . . .

Place and location of crime
. . . .

Nature of crime if not listed
above . . . .

At the foot of this, Moriarty had pencilled:

?Religion, if any . . . .
British subject by birth . . . .
Temporary immigrant . . . .
Whether paid by third party to commit the crime . . . .

Race? . . . .
By naturalization . . . .
Home Country . . . .

Roger scowled in self-criticism. He should have thought of all but the last of these, perhaps even the last, although that was one of the fundamental issues the questionnaire set out to establish. Moriarty was certainly thinking clearly.

A telephone bell rang.

'West.'

'Moriarty here, sir!' There was no doubt of the excitement in the younger man's voice. 'I'm calling you from Tottenham. The type of attack at Edmonton was the same, the area affected by the acid approximately the same, the acid almost certainly concentrated sulphuric. There will be another concentric circle to go on top of the other!'

'Was anyone caught?' demanded Roger.

'Got clear away.'

'How's the girl?'

'Pretty badly burned.'

'The man?'

'Couldn't get away fast enough, to hell with his girl.'

'Did he wash her or himself?'

'No, sir,' said Moriarty, 'but I know now why you said the other two probably realized what had happened. If you wash concentrated sulphuric acid off quickly enough it doesn't do any harm. They knew – or guessed – pretty quickly what had been sprayed on them.'

'That's right,' Roger said. 'Worth thinking about, isn't it? Is there anything else you can do out there?'

'I don't think so, sir.'

'Then call it a day,' said Roger. 'I'll be in touch tomorrow.'

'Right, sir! Goodnight.'

'Goodnight.'

Moriarty thought: He certainly thinks he knows the lot. He'll learn!

Roger rang off, stifled a yawn, and stood up to go to the window. Most of the lights were out, but the few which showed up were very bright on the river, and there was a quiet magic about the scene. A few cars moved over Westminster Bridge, headlamps dimmed and shimmering; a couple in evening dress walked hand in hand on the far side of the Embankment.

The telephone rang again.

Roger thought: Janet. She can't sleep. He crossed to his desk. 'Hallo.'

Moriarty said in a very subdued voice: 'Sorry to worry you again, sir.'

'That's all right. What is it?'

'I – er – did I leave some pencilled notes on your desk?'

Roger stifled a chuckle. 'Yes.'

'I'm sorry about that, sir, I – I meant to take them away. No discourtesy intended, sir.'

'You meant what you said, didn't you?'

'Well, yes, but I would have phrased it differently if—' Moriarty broke off. 'Anyway I'm sorry, sir.'

'I sent specimens round to each Division for suggestions,' Roger reminded him. 'In a day or two I'll find out what else I missed.'

He rang off, aware of the other's relief, just a little rueful because Moriarty apparently considered him to be very senior indeed; a kind of Elder Statesman. He yawned again. It was three o'clock, no wonder he was tired. If he took a camp bed upstairs—

Nonsense! He'd go home. He hadn't rowed with Janet; it was absurd to feel so sensitive. In this fresh mood, he grinned. After all, there had been a time not so very long ago—

He kept chuckling to himself as he drove back to Chelsea, aware of his tender shoulder but almost free from head and backache.

He felt that he was at last really at grips with the problem.

CHAPTER FIVE

'BOY' AND 'GIRL'

JANET was asleep when Roger crept into the bedroom; she stirred but did not wake. He went to sleep almost at once and slept heavily until some sound, or bright daylight, woke him. Janet's bed was empty, and made; he must have slept late. He twisted round to look at the bedside clock. It was twenty to nine, not too bad, and early for Janet to have worried about making the bed. There was stillness and silence in the house.

The boys would be gone, of course, Richard to the television studios where he worked, Martin to his art college or a round of studios and art galleries. It was the life he had chosen, but one which, so far, had not yet given him much in material returns. Roger wasn't even sure that time was on his side.

Roger got out of bed, went to the landing and called: 'Anyone about?'

There was no answer. Somewhat put out, he went downstairs to an empty kitchen and found a note by the kettle on the gas stove. He put on the kettle, then opened Janet's note.

'Sorry, darling, but I'll be out all day – the Bridge Club Outing, remember? Try not to be late tonight. There's plenty of ham and cold beef and the casserole only needs heating.'

That was true to form; and he had forgotten.

He made tea, bathed, shaved, breakfasted, all in the unaccustomed silence. No one called from the Yard, which was unusual. He had no case on hand except the main one and he would have been telephoned if anything much had developed at the Yard. The front lawn could do with a cut, but the mower, he remembered, needed attention. He put on slacks and a short-sleeved shirt, and went into the garden shed, leaving the doors open so that he could hear the telephone. It was humid and he was sweating even as he oiled and tinkered with the machine. Half an hour later, he wiped the grass off the blades and put the thing away.

'Need another bath,' he grumbled. Instead, he cooled off and dressed for the Yard, puzzled because there was no call. He wasn't used to being left alone so long, and wasn't sure that he liked it. The garage stood a little forward at one side of the house, with a narrow door at the back. The main doors were wide open – one of the boys would have done that. He sat at the wheel and started the engine.

Nothing happened; the car, like the house, seemed dead.

He pulled again, but there was no response; no whine, no sudden throb. Could the battery be flat? This *would* happen on a morning when he had already left it very late. He got out and threw up the bonnet, using his left arm with caution.

He exclaimed, 'Good Lord!'

Taped to the inside of the bonnet was a photograph, but before he did more than glance at it he looked in blank surprise at the engine. Every plug was out. The distributor head had been taken off and disconnected. The battery leads and wiring had been disconnected, too. Slowly anger replaced the surprise, and his jaw set when he looked back at the photograph.

It was the one taken of him at Young's house – his right hand, disproportionately large, raised as if to strike the man who, farthest from the camera, looked very small.

He stretched out to pull the photograph off, and then thought: Prints. He withdrew his hand, thinking bitterly that he would bet quite a large sum that the Press had been sent a copy. He went slowly indoors to telephone.

Earlier that morning, Albert Young went to get the newspaper and the post. He was not retired, but had a small boat-builder's yard, with a shop attached for supplying small craft with their needs. Over the years he had added picnic oddments and some gardening and household goods to the stock. He had once had a partner, but had split up years before. Now he and his wife ran the business with occasional help from Helena. He did just as much work as he wanted, when he wanted, preferring to work late at night rather than in the early morning, He had slept very heavily once he had got off, and had been awake only for ten minutes.

His wife was still in bed.

Heavy-hearted, bitter, sulking and angry, he picked up letters and papers from the mat, yawned, and carried them into the kitchen. He put on the kettle, then turned to the newspapers – and saw a glossy photograph sticking out of the pages of one of them. He pulled it further out, then stared down, his body rigidly at attention.

It was the photograph of a man – the back of a man – near-naked.

And his daughter's face, eyes wide in terror, distorted; beyond any doubt Helena's.

Slowly, almost painfully, Young's lips moved.

'The harlot,' he said distinctly. 'The *har*lot.'

Then he carried the photograph into the bedroom, and shook his wife awake.

Roger reached the Yard at a quarter to twelve and realized

almost at once that there was an atmosphere – and that he was the subject of more attention than usual; everyone went out of their way to acknowledge him. He turned into his own office to find several notes on the desk, as well as the usual crop of files – and at least a dozen of the questionnaires. The messages were all brief. 'Commander Coppell called.' 'Superintendent Davey of North Central Division called.' 'Commander Coppell wants you to call him.' 'Chief Inspector Moriarty called.' 'Superintendent Windlesham of Charlton called.' 'Commander Coppell would like to see you – urgently.' He sat down and called Coppell's office; a woman secretary said:

'Who's that ... ?'

'Superintendent West.'

'Oh, thank goodness, Mr West!'

'Am I still wanted?'

'Yes, at *once*.'

Roger said: 'I'm on my way. Why didn't you call me at home?'

'We understood you'd been injured, Mr West.'

'Oh.' He rang off and went down one flight of stairs, reached the landing near Coppell's office and was stopped by a Superintendent carrying an early edition of the *Evening Globe*.

'Seen this, Handsome!'

The paper was thrust into Roger's face. 'This' was a photograph – the one he had received that morning. The caption read: *Superintendent West at Acid Victim's Home*. He wrinkled his nose.

'Were you going to hit him or was it self-defence?' the other man asked.

'Neither,' said Roger tartly.

He went into Coppell's office as the secretary, tall, prim, wearing spectacles with pale rims, came out of the doorway leading to the inner sanctum.

'Oh, Mr West.' She looked over her shoulder. 'Mr West is here, sir.'

'Send him in.'

Coppell, a heavy, dark-featured man, sat behind a big square-topped desk. Like his immediate predecessor, Hardy, he had risen from the ranks, and fitted rather awkwardly into the position of senior executive detective at the Yard. He was always a little too well-shaven, his hair was too perfectly cut and trimmed, his clothes too well-fitting.

'Sit down,' he said. 'Thought you were hurt.'

'It was exaggerated,' Roger remarked.

After a pause, Coppell slid a copy of the *Evening Globe* across the desk.

'Get it doing this?'

Roger said carefully: 'Immediately afterwards.'

'Did you have to get rough with this man Young?'

'I didn't get rough with him.'

'Camera playing tricks?' asked Coppell.

The remark was almost jocular, coming from him, but Roger felt a surge of anger. Why should Coppell jump to that conclusion? A possibility dawned on him suddenly.

'Was there a letter with the newspaper?' he asked.

'Yes,' said Coppell, 'it was brought in by an errand boy who said a man had given him half a crown to deliver it. The writer wanted to know if this was how we browbeat our witnesses.'

'Anonymous, I presume,' Roger said acidly.

Coppell's frown became a scowl; after a pause, he pushed a handwritten scrawl across his desk and Roger reached for it with his left arm, winced, and edged himself forward on his chair. He read it and the signature, A. Young, tossed it back and said:

'Sure it's Young's writing?'

'Isn't it?' Coppell barked.

'I doubt it very much,' Roger said. 'It shouldn't be hard to find out.' He fell silent, waiting, and Coppell now appeared to glower. It was a strangely tense pause and in it Roger realized that the situation could become serious – Coppell was the boss. He shifted back in his chair, forcing himself to relax, to explain reasonably all that had happened. He mentioned Moriarty's call, and went on: 'If there *is* a gang, it either works in groups, or the gang split up last night – the same man couldn't have taken that photograph and thrown the acid on the couple at Edmonton.'

Coppell rubbed his chin.

'No.' He paused. '*Are* you badly hurt?'

'My shoulder's stiff, that's all. I was late last night, and my wife let me sleep in.'

'Sensible woman,' said Coppell heartily, obviously accepting the olive branch. 'What do you make of the overall picture? Think any of the attacks were connected?'

'I doubt it,' answered Roger, 'but it could be. More likely some of these young bloods think it would be a lark to have a go.'

'*Lark!*' echoed Coppell. 'Is throwing acid what you call a lark?'

'It might seem funny to a certain type of practical joker or to anyone with a lewd sense of humour,' Roger reasoned. 'We may get a lead either from Wainwright, who's in hospital, or from the Chelsea victim who disappeared. Both probably knew that concentrated sulphuric acid was used, or they wouldn't have rushed for water. There could be two opposing gangs or two factions of the same gang having a fight, and the victims could be members of one or the other. I'll tackle Wainwright as soon as I can about it. Also, we might get a lead from the youth who was caught at Shepherd's Bush – I'll go and see him myself.'

'Better hurry,' said Coppell. 'He's going to be charged to-day, and the court's very busy – Division asks you to be there by one o'clock at the latest.'

It was ten past twelve.

'I'd better be on my way then. Is that all, sir?'

'For the present, yes. Any replies in from your questionnaires?'

'A few – I haven't examined them yet, though.' Roger got up, approached the door, and then exclaimed: 'Good Lord! I forgot to tell you about my car . . .'

Coppell listened, his frown thunderous, and when Roger had finished he said:

'So they've declared war on us, have they?'

'Or on me personally.'

'Well, don't let them win.'

Roger said mechanically: 'Not if I can help it.' He reached the door. 'It might be a good idea to have young Moriarty transferred here from the Division, sir. May I promise Division a replacement, if necessary?'

'Yes,' said Coppell. 'Let me know what you decide.' He stood up, abruptly. 'And give this acid-throwing job top priority. We don't want to be made a laughing stock.'

Laughing stock, Roger repeated to himself as he got into the back of a car and a driver closed the door on him. He sat back and narrowed his eyes. *Laughing stock.* Some people would find the acid throwing, in these circumstances, hilariously funny, people with a streak of sadism in their make-up. Others would find the lesser incidents funny. Someone had tried to make a fool of him over the car and over the photograph and letter – unless Albert Young *had* written to the Yard. The more he thought of that the more unlikely it seemed. *Laughing stock.* 'They've declared war on *us*,' Coppell had said. Certainly nothing would tickle the palate of the public more than failure to solve this particular problem quickly. On the one hand there were those who would be shocked and horrified at the crime, and on the other, those who saw in it a stern example of Old Testament justice. Both sides would write in belabouring the inefficiency of the police. Roger saw that if he wasn't careful he would easily find himself side-tracked away from the main issue, – the CRIMINAL ACTIVITY OF YOUNG PEOPLE.

Was it – could it conceivably be a deliberate attempt to distract the police from a series of crimes?

Having voiced the question, he could hardly justify it even to himself. All he knew was that it had come to mind.

He opened the questionnaire folder and glanced through. All except one of a dozen Divisions which had answered wanted *Race* and *Religion* included; but there was nothing new of any importance. By the time he had finished, the car was turning into the narrow street where the Shepherd's Bush Divisional Headquarters was housed.

The Superintendent of the Station, Ellis, was a tall, pale, cold-mannered man, a little peeved at the late hour of Roger's arrival. The magistrate was becoming restive, he hadn't expected an afternoon sitting. The prisoner had refused to say a word, and evidence of his identification had not been forthcoming.

'Doesn't he, himself, give a name?' asked Roger.

'Not really – calls himself John Smith.'

'I suppose he *could* be John Smith,' Roger mused, and won an expression of distaste. 'May I go and see him?'

Ellis said: 'I'll send an Inspector down with you.'

The cells were well lit yet oddly sinister. The rattle and clink of the duty officer's keys seemed very loud. The youth sitting on a narrow bed had long, fair hair and an unexpectedly sensitive face, with fine brown eyes, and upsweeping lashes. He sat motionless until the door opened – and then leapt to his feet and hurled himself across the cell in a desperate but futile effort to escape.

CHAPTER SIX

COURT HEARING

ROGER and the Detective Inspector who had come with him moved almost by reflex action to bar the youth's path. The duty officer in the passage slammed the door. As it clanged to, the youth turned on the Inspector and began to kick and strike at him in senseless fury. Roger closed with him from behind. The youth gasped and fell back. His eyes were wild, his teeth showed as his lips curled.

Roger said to the duty officer: 'Get a doctor.'

'Yes, sir!'

'Doctor,' growled the Inspector, a bony man with shiny cheeks and high cheekbones. 'He wants a straitjacket.'

The youth was now standing beside the bed, quivering all over. As the man in the passage hurried off Roger took out cigarettes and proffered them; the youth took one, shakily. Roger offered the packet to the other man, who grunted:

'I don't smoke.'

Roger flicked a lighter for the prisoner, who drew deeply on the cigarette. He should have been given cigarettes before. No one as yet had taken much trouble with this youth. He appeared healthy enough, thin, but by no means emaciated. Roger sat down on the bed.

'What had young Cobden done to offend you?'

'Who?'

'Cobden.'

'Who's Cobden?'

'Betty Smith's boy-friend.'

'Betty? Who's Bet—' began the youth, and then broke off and moistened the end of his cigarette. 'Those kids.'

'Yes.'

'It was – it was just fun, a lark.'

41

'Lark!' echoed the Detective Inspector.

'You mean you didn't know them?'

'Hell, no.'

'Why attack them?'

'I tell you, it was just a lark.'

'Who were the others?'

'What others?'

'The couple with you.'

The youth rolled the cigarette from one side of his mouth to the other.

'Just pals.'

'Out for a lark?'

'Yes.'

'How often do you have that kind of lark?'

The youth said thinly: 'When we're in the mood, see. If you think I'm going to give my pals away you've another think coming.'

'They'll look after you, will they? They'll be in court, with a lawyer to speak up for you and explain it was just a lark.'

'That's what it was.'

'What's your name?' Roger asked casually.

'Find out!'

Roger laughed. 'That won't be difficult. One photograph in a newspaper or on television, and plenty of people will come forward to identify you. Why waste our time and put everyone to a lot of trouble?'

The youth said stubbornly: 'My name's John Smith.'

'Where do you live?'

'Find out.'

In the silence which followed, footsteps sounded, and the duty officer and a very young man of medium height appeared, the middle-aged officer breathing heavily. He unlocked the cell door, and the doctor came in, glanced curiously at Roger, and then asked:

'What's the trouble?'

'I'd like to make sure he's fit to plead,' Roger said.

'It will take hours to find out.'

'I mean whether he can stand up to five minutes in the dock.'

'It's obvious—' began the Detective Inspector, but subsided at a glance from Roger.

The doctor felt 'John Smith's pulse, put a stethoscope on his chest, looked into his eyes with an ophthalmoscope, and then put his instruments away.

'Five or fifty minutes in dock won't do him any harm,' he said with owlish certainty.

'Anyone could have told it was an act,' the Inspector said, under his breath.

Roger glared and the youth glowered back.

Twenty minutes later he came up the stairs below the dock, with a warder behind him and a policeman close by. The Press box was full, and there was an air of tension, though half a dozen people sat in the public seats. A police inspector was waiting to take the oath, impatient during the preliminaries. The magistrate, elderly, sandy-haired, looked strangely shrunken against the dark panelled background of the bench.

'. . . what's his name?'

'Given as John Smith,' the magistrate's clerk said.

'Hm. I seem to have heard that name before.' There were a few dutiful titters about the court. 'Has John Smith anything to say about the charge of assault?'

'No, your honour.'

The youth looked down at the brass rail in front of him.

'Evidence of arrest, please,' said the magistrate.

A young constable who had been in the well of the court took the oath and deposed formally on the arrest on a charge of causing bodily harm, and as he talked Roger saw the prisoner look up from under his lashes. The witness stepped down and the Inspector took his place.

'. . . and if it please your honour we would like a remand in custody to complete our inquiries. We hope . . .'

'Very well.' The magistrate looked severely at the prisoner. 'You, John Smith, are remanded for eight days and at the expiration of that period I advise you to be legally represented, and to enter a formal plea, and—'

'*Watch him!*' cried Roger.

The prisoner suddenly gripped the bar, and vaulted over the front of the dock, evading the warder who tried to grab him. He banged heavily into a startled policeman, and leapt towards the bench.

During the short, sharp mêlée which followed, the

magistrate sat waiting with praiseworthy calm, until the prisoner was pinioned only a foot or two in front of him.

'I order that the accused be examined medically during the period of remand,' he said. 'Remove him, please.'

The cynical Detective Inspector muttered unsteadily: 'You expected something like that, sir, didn't you?'

'Half-expected it,' Roger said. 'We don't want to take any risks – if a prisoner is violent either because he can't help it or because he's putting on an act, we want a medical check at once.'

'Do you really think he's a medical case, sir?'

'If he's not I want to know why he's putting on this act,' Roger answered.

'Just for a lark, maybe,' the other remarked, with a grim inflection.

'Much more likely he's terrified. I want to know why,' Roger said, and he thought: *lark? ... lark? ...*

Roger was driven to Wimbledon, going through Hammersmith Broadway, past the grimy shops and small houses of Fulham Palace Road, over the broad sweep of the bridge across the Thames at Putney, seeing the shimmering expanse of the river on either side; two fours were starting from the very spot from which the Oxford and Cambridge Boat Race began every year, and a few dozen people strolled in the sun along the tow-path. Not far along, although he did not yet know it, was Albert Young's shop. He sat back as they went up Putney Hill, and near The Green Man at Putney Heath the radio woke.

'Calling Inspector West.'

There was a receiver at the back of the car. Roger lifted it off.

'West speaking.'

'There's a message from Chief Inspector Moriarty of Wimbledon, sir. He is at the Windmill and would appreciate it if you will go there.'

'Tell him I'll be with him in ten minutes or so.'

'Right, sir.'

'Is Superintendent Sloane there?'

'I'll see, sir.' There was a short pause, before another man spoke laconically. 'Sloane here.'

'I want a general request to all Divisions for word about any man named Lark who is associated with Youth Clubs or similar organizations. Fix it on the teletype, will you?'

'I will, sir. I seem to have heard the name in that connection.'

'So do I, but I can't place him,' said Roger.

He rang off, leaned back, and looked at the new houses and the blocks of flats where Victorian mansions had once stood alongside the common. The whole road had changed a great deal since his own youth, but the common side was little different, and still dense with foliage. Narrow lanes led off through trees and bushes, as the driver slowed down for the turning which led to the Windmill. A police car with a uniformed man at attention was standing by. He came forward.

'I'll lead the way to Mr Moriarty, sir.'

Roger nodded.

The two cars drove jerkily over uneven grassland, with cars and pedestrians milling about in close confusion as the police cleared a way to the cordoned off area. This was a patch of common-land dotted with bushes and saplings, and a thick tangle of bramble. Roger walked towards it as Moriarty appeared, authoritative-looking in the bright sunlight.

'Good afternoon, sir.'

'What have you found?' demanded Roger.

'Three more footprints; we're taking casts of them,' answered Moriarty. 'And this, sir.'

He held out a small book of matches which had been trampled on and creased, but the printed wording was easily readable. It said:

You get the best fun at the Lark Club.

Roger turned it over and opened it, seeing a few red-topped matches but no other lettering, no address.

'Fingerprints?'

'None, sir.'

'Odd.'

'No way of being sure how long it's been here,' Moriarty said, 'but I think since last night – almost sure, in fact.'

'What makes you sure?'

'It was on top of one of the footprints.'

'So all we need to be certain of is that the footprints were made last night,' Roger said. 'Have you seen the photographs?'

'Yes,' said Moriarty, and added grimly: 'Albert Young had one, too.'

Roger said heavily: 'Did he? Do you have a specimen of his handwriting?'

'No.'

'I'd like one quickly,' Roger said. 'What about his daughter?'

'She's still at the hospital.' Moriarty put the book of matches into a cellophane envelope, with great care. 'And he's still the Victorian father. I've finished here, sir. Unless you want to—'

Roger said: 'Let's go down and see Young.'

There was no way of being sure that Young would receive them pleasantly or even civilly, and when Roger saw a dozen gaping sightseers, his heart dropped; Young might not even open the door. But he did, and Roger was shocked by the dark rings beneath his eyes, the evidence of sleeplessness, the pain which showed so clearly.

'If I answer your questions will you get this – this pack of *hyenas* off my doorstep?' he demanded.

'We'll do all we can to make sure you're not harassed,' Roger promised. They went in, and as the door closed he asked: 'Why did you send that newspaper photograph to Scotland Yard, Mr Young?'

In the doorway of a little front room, Young turned his head.

'*I* didn't send any photograph anywhere. I tore the beastly thing up.'

Roger said: 'Isn't this your handwriting?' and he held out the letter Coppell had shown him. Young glanced at it, and then marched straight into the room and picked up a half-finished letter from a small writing desk. 'There's *my* writing,' he barked. 'Does it look the same?'

It could hardly have been more dissimilar; the letter was a scrawl, the writing on the desk was beautifully clear and neat, obviously written with pride. It was on headed paper which read: *Albert Young, Boatbuilder – Ship's Chandler*. Young appeared satisfied with Roger's expression, then looked at the other signature again, and asked as if wonderingly: 'Who on earth would want to pretend that was me?'

'We'll find out,' Roger said. 'Do you know anyone named Lark, Mr Young?'

'Lark? *Lark?*' Young pondered, and then answered. 'I used to know a boy named Lark at school – must be thirty-five years since I saw him.'

'Have you ever heard your daughter mention the Lark Club?'

'No, I haven't. *And* I never want to hear my daughter mentioned again.'

'I'm sorry you feel like that, sir. I'm sure she would value your help very much.' Roger paused. 'To your knowledge, has she any friends – men friends – who might be excessively jealous?'

'*I* don't know her friends. She rejected my advice years ago, and her mother encouraged her in her independence. As she never took any notice of me, there was no point in saying anything to her, was there? For all I know, there might have been a dozen of these sordid affairs.'

'Do you think your wife might be able to help me?' asked Roger impatiently.

'She may. She's at the hospital, and I have no idea when she will be back. In fact she might decide to go and stay with relations. I—' Young paused, and cocked his head. 'There's her key in the door now,' he said. 'If you wish to question her, please use the other room.'

He moved to the door, but before he reached the passage someone came hurrying, and over his grey head Roger saw a girl with a bandaged forehead and some patches on her cheeks, but young and obviously attractive. Before Young or anyone else could speak, she cried:

'Is Mummy here? *Is she here?* She ran away from the hospital saying she would rather kill herself than suffer like this. *Is she here?*'

CHAPTER SEVEN

'LARK'

As father and daughter stood facing each other, bitter and hostile, Roger moved to Moriarty and whispered:

'Do you know what Mrs Young looks like?'

'Yes.'

'Get out a general call, through this and neighbouring Divisions,' Roger said. 'Rivers, ponds – you know the drill.'

'Right!' Moriarty pushed past the girl towards the front door. Both man and daughter were talking, the girl in a high-pitched, near-hysterical tone, the man almost growling, but none of the words had registered on Roger as he had given the instructions. Now the words took shape.

'. . . it's your fault, it's all your fault!'

'Don't you dare raise your voice at me!'

'If she kills herself, her death will be on *your* conscience,' the girl screamed. 'You've driven her to it!'

'If she kills herself it will be out of the shame you've brought on to your parents and your home.'

'It's your fault – oh, God, oh God, *where is she*?' The girl spun round, seized Roger, and cried: 'Can't you find her? Can't you go and look for her?'

'We've already started a search. We'll find her,' Roger promised confidently. 'Oughtn't you to be in hospital?'

'I had to come out, I had to look for her!'

'If your mother dies of shame it will be on *your* conscience,' Young said in a deep, carrying voice, almost as if he were declaiming from a pulpit; give him a beard and he would look like an Old Testament prophet, threatening the people with hellfire. 'Leave this house before shame destroys us all.'

Helena caught her breath as if seized by a sudden, unbearable spasm. She had the most beautiful velvety blue eyes, untouched by the acid, and her lips were unscarred, too. They quivered uncontrollably, her whole body seemed to quiver.

'You heard me,' her father said.

'You – you mean it,' she said in a tremulous voice. 'You really mean it. And you *did* drive mother away. You—'

She broke off, catching her voice again, and as she stared at her father, Moriarty returned, lips parted to speak. He checked himself. The silence seemed to last for a long time, before the girl said in a husky voice:

'Daddy, please, *please* don't take it out on Mummy. Do what you like to me, but don't hurt Mummy.'

Young said mercilessly: 'Your mother has her choice, I will not make it for her. And nor will you.'

'No!' Helena gasped. 'You can't be so – wicked. You *can't*

be so wicked.' When her father simply stood and returned her stare, tears filled her eyes.

'What's happened to you?' she cried. 'What's changed you? You used to be so – so kind.'

'You used to be my daughter.'

There was another moment of utter silence before the girl spun round and ran out of the room. Roger saw Moriarty move almost on the instant and go after her; her footsteps, then his, sounded clearly along the passage and on the porch. Young stared at the open door, hard-faced, his hands clenched by his side, his eyes – so like his daughter's – burning as if in pain. The anger and the disgust which had built up in Roger slowly died and he felt a strange pity for this man.

Quietly he said: 'We will find your wife, Mr Young, and I don't think you need worry. When a woman's worked up, a threat of suicide doesn't mean very much. Will you be in all the afternoon?'

Young did not answer.

'Will you, sir?'

Young did not even glance at him, it was doubtful if he had heard a word.

Roger left him and went to the front door. The crowd had grown to thirty or forty people, and one man at the front had a camera; at times the Press seemed like ghouls. The camera clicked. Moriarty was talking to a plainclothes man at the side of a police car; the girl was not in sight. One policeman was at the wheel, another stood in the doorway; Roger beckoned him and they backed into the hall as the car moved off.

'Do you know this street?'

'It's on my regular beat, sir.'

'Know anything about Young and his neighbours?'

'He's got no friends locally, sir – Mrs Young has, but not Young as far as I know. He's gone a bit – well, a bit fanatical lately.'

'On his own?'

'Yes, sir – he doesn't belong to any particular sect, if that's what you mean.'

Roger persisted: 'He must have *some* friends.'

'Well – he used to have a partner, a Mr Josephs, in a kind of ship's chandler business just near the river. Now he's on his own. Young does a bit in garden supplies too, oils, provisions for week-enders on the river. Not much of a business, but he gets along. Josephs has his own business too, but they're still on speaking terms. They used to be close friends but Young got funny, a few years ago, and put everyone against him.'

'What's Josephs like?'

'Pretty sound chap, sir.'

'Think he'd let bygones be bygones now?'

'I'll go and have a word with him, if you like,' the policeman said. He was in his late fifties and looked his age – and there was an understanding gentleness in his manner. 'Think there's any risk of *him* trying to do away with himself?'

'You can never tell.'

'I'll hurry, sir,' the policeman said.

Roger went back into the house. Albert Young was sitting at the writing desk, hands resting on it, staring at a calendar just above eye level, a picture of a Thameside scene at the top. His eyes seemed sunken as well as burning, now – as if *he* were suffering the torment of fire and brimstone.

'We'll let you know when we've news of your wife,' Roger promised gently.

There was nothing to indicate that Young heard him.

Roger turned and went out. Moriarty could leave a man here, or send a neighbour, or for a doctor. The problem was to decide where responsibility left off, but preventing a suicide was a police responsibility, clearly enough.

A man called from Moriarty's car: 'They've located Mrs Young, sir!'

'Is she hurt?' demanded Moriarty sharply.

Agnes Young only knew that there was a suffocating feeling in her breast and strange, confused pictures, and knife-like pains in her head. She had sat with her daughter in the hospital for an hour, while the pains got worse, and then she had jumped up, saying:

'I must go now, dear. You'll be all right, don't worry.'

She realized that her manner must seem strange to Helena, but could not help it; she only knew that she must get away. As she rushed out of the ward, she muttered under her breath: *'I'll kill myself. It's the only thing left.'* A patient, half-dozing, heard her. Along a wide passage, walking quickly and blindly, she said: *'He'll never take her back. Never. And I*

50

won't go back on my own. I'll kill myself, that's what I'll do.'

A little Jamaican ward nurse heard her.

Behind her there was a swell of gossip and alarm which was carried back to her daughter, but before this happened she was out in the street. Cars screeched interminably. Lorries roared deafeningly past. A bus bore down on her like a monster with a gaping mouth. Noise, noise, noise. It seemed to draw her towards it and yet at the same time repulsed her. *Noise, noise noise.* It was like Albert's voice, deep, grating, remorseless. 'She is no longer my daughter. If you wish to see her you must leave this house. I tell you I forbid you to see her again. She is a harlot.'

Harlot, harlot, harlot—

Noise, noise, noise, noise.

Roar, roar, roar, roar.

Wheels going round, red monsters passing, brakes squealing, men shouting. Noise, noise, noise. A man came to her and touched her and let her go. Noise . . . noise . . . noise . . . It was fading. It was softer.

'Mummy, I'm sorry, oh, I'm so sorry . . . I love him . . . I do love him . . . I didn't mean . . . Mummy, please don't cry, Daddy doesn't mean it, he can't mean it.'

Daddy, daddy, daddy, Albert, Albert, Albert, noise, noise, noise.

In front of her was the river, broad and smooth and inviting, the only sound the lapping of water against the bank. A few pieces of driftwood swayed past, a jetty with a broken rail. Come, come, come, the water will stop the pain, the water will soothe you. Come, come, come. The water was beautiful and cool, up to her ankles, her knees, her waist, cool, soothing. She heard noises, voices, shouting, whistling, but all noise like all fear and all distress was behind her now. The water was up to her breast, lapping against her chin.

Everything will be all right now.

A face appeared in front of her, the face of a man, swimming. Suddenly, other men appeared in a boat, almost alongside.

'Careful.' 'She'll be all right.' 'Watch her.' 'Let me help you, ma'am.' 'Let me help—'

They were going to take her away from this wonderful coolness, this peace. She realized that, and went wild with fear and rage and some deeper emotion she could not understand. All the repressed despair of the past months swept over her. She struck a face, struck an oar, the water closed over her and she gulped it down, her eyes were open but she could not see, she knew hands were clutching her but she could not feel, she kicked and gulped and felt her lungs filling. She did not know when the men in the boat hauled her out of the water while the swimming man stayed near.

'All right, is she?' Roger asked.

'They pulled her out of the river,' said the man at the radio. 'She came round after artificial respiration.'

'Where is she?'

'In an ambulance on the way to the hospital.'

'Best place for her.' Roger turned to Moriarty, who was close by, and said: 'That family's in a pretty bad way.'

'Living with such a couple must have been hell for the daughter,' Moriarty observed.

'Wonder how long it's been going on?'

'Too long.'

'Where's the girl?'

Moriarty hesitated, and then seemed to draw himself up to attention as he said very formally:

'I thought she should go somewhere comfortable and where no one will tell her she brought it all on herself, sir. I've sent her to my place.'

'Your place!'

'Don't misunderstand me,' Moriarty added with great dignity. 'I have a small service flat in a converted house, and the landlady lives on the premises and does for me. There's a spare room, but not in my apartment, sir. She'll be well looked after.'

'I'm sure she will,' said Roger gently. 'Don't become too involved though – it could lead to complications.'

Who's he to tell me what I can do? Moriarty asked himself, I can do what *I* think's best. I'm not allowing anyone, Superintendent or no Superintendent, to tell me what to do in my private life.

'What's known about Helena Young's boy-friend?' Roger

asked. He could not understand the expression on Moriarty's face but thought there was a sulky kind of self-defence, almost of defiance.

'He's Anthony Wainwright from Cairns, Queensland. Been over here for three years – he's an agent for some firm of costume jewellery and does quite well, I gather. Nothing known about him, except—'

'Yes?'

'Bit of a womanizer, according to reports, the kind girls *say* they're very careful about.'

'Oh.'

'No doubt at all Helena Young thought he was serious over her,' went on Moriarty.

'Have you seen him?' asked Roger.

'Only for a few minutes – and he wasn't allowed to talk. The doctors said he could this afternoon.'

'I'll go and see him,' Roger said. He paused and then asked: 'Are you particularly attached to the Division?'

Moriarty seemed to draw himself up and become very formal again; it was hard to say whether this was a pose, or natural.

'It's pretty good as Divisions go, sir. Of course, I would much rather be at—' he broke off, his eyes widened, he gave that unexpectedly boyish smile, and then he waited, almost breathlessly.

Roger had a feeling that there was something forced about his manner.

'I'd find you very useful at the Yard for this job,' Roger said. 'Like me to find out what your Superintendent thinks, or will you apply yourself?'

'I'll apply, sir – thanks! This is the chance I've been waiting for!'

'Yes,' Roger said. 'And working for, no doubt.' He did not add that it was the kind of chance which could go sour on a man; that work at the Yard was very different from work at the Divisions. He hoped Moriarty wouldn't need telling that other, older officers at the Yard might feel sensitive about a young man coming in on this kind of special assignment. Moriarty's eyes were glowing, and it seemed a pity to do anything which might dampen his enthusiasm.

'I'll go and see Wainwright,' Roger decided.

He doesn't approve but he won't stop me, Moriarty thought when Roger had gone. He knows he can't handle this job himself, and needs me, but he'll take the credit – *if* I let him. Good thing I can handle him without his realizing it.

Wainwright was in a small private ward, lying on his right side, away from the light and also away from the detective who sat with him all the time. Roger sent the man out, and rounded the bed. Wainwright, who had the radio phone clipped to his ear, pretended not to notice Roger as he pulled up a chair and sat down. The man's face was unscathed, but patches had been shaved in his hair, and plastered over. He had a long, unusual face, with finely marked features and eyebrows; a Valentino of a man, obviously not of English stock.

'Congratulations,' Roger said.

Wainwright opened his eyes wider.

'For what?'

'Playing a hero's part.'

Wainwright grimaced.

'I'm no hero. You can't take a girl for a lay and then let some baskets mutilate her. How is the little doll?'

Roger felt dislike for the man hardening, yet felt a touch of admiration, too.

'Worried. About her parents, I gather.'

'Parents. So what?' Wainwright took the ear phone off, moving very cautiously. 'They'll get over it, and she'll suffer less permanent harm than I will. I'm going to have a lot of trouble explaining these scars to my lady friends. Who are you?'

'Superintendent West. Mr Wainwright, have you ever heard of the Lark Club?'

The question was uttered casually but Roger was on the watch for the slightest reaction – already convinced that this man might well be a practised liar, and one who could keep a poker face far better than most.

Instead, Wainwright almost exploded.

'*That* outfit! I've heard of it, tried it, and dumped it overboard. Don't make me laugh. It hurts too much.'

'Here's something that won't prove too amusing,' Roger said drily. 'What made you so certain you'd been sprayed with sulphuric acid? Were the sprayers friends of yours?'

Wainwright's expression changed to one of blank disinterest.

'I happen to know about sulphuric acid,' he answered, 'and I'd read about some cases of spraying in the papers. I just didn't take any chances.'

That was all he would say, but Roger suspected that he knew a great deal more.

CHAPTER EIGHT

WORD OF JOSIAH LARK

ROGER returned to the Yard soon after five o'clock to find his desk piled high with returned questionnaires, reports about the four cases on the previous night, and newspapers with copies of the picture of him 'threatening' Young. There were other pictures of the Cobden boy and Betty Smith, of Jill Hickersley, who had been attacked in Chelsea, and the couple who had been attacked in Edmonton – cousins named Abbott. The picture here was of a remarkably beautiful girl and a surprisingly homely young man. Attached to the photographs were typewritten reports, each signed with the initials: *B.M.* The typing was perfect; Moriarty must have laid on a typist very quickly. Roger ran through all of the reports, finding that of the Abbotts particularly interesting. They were older than anyone else involved, but still young – in the middle twenties. The girl, now so greviously hurt, lived with three other young women in a flat; the man lived with his parents in an overcrowded house.

Roger rang for a messenger.

'Get me some tea and sandwiches, right away.'

'Yes, sir.'

'And find out if Chief Inspector Moriarty is in the building.'

'Oh, he is, sir.'

'Send him in to me, will you?'

Roger frowned as the door closed; it was one thing to be on the ball, another to jump the gun. Was Moriarty jumping the gun? There was a tap at the door, and he came in almost too soon. The expression of aggressive alertness was very noticeable; this man lived in a perpetual state of nervous tension which in itself might create problems.

'You didn't lose much time,' Roger remarked drily.

'Mr Davis said the quicker I vacated an office for a replacement at Division the better,' Moriarty said, 'and I know Bill – Chief Inspector Evans – very well.' Evans was one of the younger officers at the Yard. 'So I left my files with him and he showed me around.'

'How's the Young girl?' Roger asked.

'I don't know anything more about her, sir. Her mother's all right, though she's suffering from shock. And an old friend of the father has turned up. Young's with him now. The affair has absolutely split that family wide open.'

Roger said: 'I wonder how many other families are living close to a break-up.' He stood up and moved to the window. 'What have we really got here, so far?' He pointed to his reports.

'Crime-wise, sir?' asked Moriarty.

'Any-wise.'

'Except for the Smith/Cobden affair, all the young people involved seem to be living out of touch with their parents,' replied Moriarty. 'I've been trying to find a common factor – apart from young love!' He gave a quick, smothered grin. 'Haven't yet, sir!' When Roger appeared to wait for him to go on, he added: 'What did you make of Wainwright?'

'A womanizer.'

'Oh. Doesn't he care for Helena Young?'

'If he does he's putting up a good act,' Roger said. 'The one thing he was helpful about was the Lark Club. Apparently it's a social club in Kensington run by a Josiah Lark, with the idea of getting young people together in ideal and highly moral surroundings. No bedrooms but no rigid rules and regulations. Ever heard of it before?'

'I have a feeling I've read about it,' Moriarty said. 'The name rings a bell.'

'Division knows of it but nothing against it,' Roger said. 'It's been heard of by two or three other Divisions, but that's all. The address is Mountjoy Street, South Kensington – have a look at it, will you?'

'Yes, sir.'

There was a tap at the door and the messenger brought in Roger's tea and two large ham sandwiches. As he put them down on a small table Roger was tempted to ask Moriarty to join him; but that slight reservation he felt about the other stifled the impulse.

'Who's your typist?' he asked.

'*I* am,' said Moriarty promptly.

'Touch typist?'

'Yes, sir – and my shorthand will stand up, too.'

'Very useful indeed.' Roger crossed to the table. 'By tomorrow we'll have somewhere for you to work, and we'll really get down to this job.'

'Can't be too soon for me,' Moriarty said and moved towards the door. 'What time will you be leaving the office?'

'Not for at least an hour.'

'I'll be with Chief Inspector Evans if you want me, sir,' said Moriarty, and he went out briskly.

He certainly thinks he's the real McCoy, Moriarty thought as he went out. These Yard types always do, but he's the bloody limit. Didn't even offer me a cup of tea, he's so anxious to rub in his superiority. He'll soon find out. It's ability that counts, not rank. 'Handsome' West is riding for a fall!

Roger sat down, drank a cup of tea, enjoyed the sandwiches, and pondered most casually. A great deal had happened in the past twenty-four hours and it would be easy to get some things out of perspective – including Moriarty. It was essential at this stage to keep a sense of proportion. He was making a survey of crime, he must remember, not of morals or social behaviour generally. Only where they caused crime could he allow himself to take an active interest.

Certain facts were hard and fast; and these he put down on a notepad, in pencil.

1. Acid throwing was a crime.
2. Assault as at Chelsea, Wimbledon, and Edmonton was a crime.
3. 'John Smith' had committed a crime.
4. 'John Smith' had talked about it being 'just a lark'.
5. The Lark Club book of matches had been found on the scene at Wimbledon Common.
6. Wainwright both knew and derided the club.

7. Nothing was known against the club or its owner.

8. The attack on Wainwright and Helena Young had caused one attempted suicide. How many other people were being affected indirectly?

9. There was no apparent connection between any of the couples victimized.

10. There was no identification of the assailants but there were indications (according to Moriarty) that the acid spraying might have been done by the same person.

11. The photograph at Young's house showed that either he, Superintendent Roger West, had been followed, which wasn't likely, or that the assailants on the common had been watching Young's house – and in many ways this was the most puzzling factor.

12. The attempts to discredit him, Roger, by sending the photograph to the Yard could mean that his, Roger's, investigations had touched a sore spot somewhere. On the other hand, it could have been impersonal malice.

Roger pushed the notepad away from him, and went to the window, gazing with unseeing eyes at the familiar panoramic view. These were the known facts, and all manner of questions arose out of them. The first and probably the most important was: were the different *kinds* of assault connected, or were they imitative? It was odd that 'John Smith', whose assault in its way had been less serious than any of the others, should have used that rather out-dated word 'lark'. Had it been just a phrase? Why had he insisted on keeping his name back anyhow? Why had he made those two attempts to escape – both almost futile from the beginning. Was he a little odd in the head, or did he want to create just that impression?

A telephone rang – the outside line. Roger moved across.

'West.'

'There's a Mr Pengelly on the line asking for you, sir. Pengelly of the *Daily Globe*.'

That Pengelly. 'Put him on.' *That* Pengelly was a middle-aged reporter whom Roger had known for twenty years. That he worked for the most sensational of the dailies did not alter the fact that he was highly responsible in his approach to his job.

'Handsome?'

'Hallo, Pen. How are you?'

'Outraged,' said Pengelly. 'By all these shocking goings on.'

'So are we all,' said Roger. 'What have you got for me?'

'A certain Mr John Smith Walter Osgood,' announced Pengelly bluffly.

Without, at first, recognizing the significance of the name, Roger echoed: 'John Smith Walter – oh!'

'That's right,' said Pengelly. 'I've just been into the City Police Headquarters in Old Jewry and saw a picture of your "John Smith". He is, in fact, Walter Osgood – I'm quite sure of that. He is the one who was remanded at Shepherd's Bush this afternoon, isn't he?'

'Yes.'

'Peculiar,' remarked Pengelly.

'Must you be so obscure?'

'He's such a *good* young man,' Pengelly elaborated sarcastically. 'Or he's supposed to be. Quite a leading light in some Youth Club movements.' Pengelly was an active Youth Club worker and the *Evening Globe* as well as the *Daily Globe*, the morning paper of the group, sponsored a number of such clubs in the London area; there were *Globe* tennis tournaments, swimming, table tennis, cricket, football, and netball competitions. The *Globe* believed in getting among the people. So did Pengelly, who had a remarkable nose for the unlikely and romantic story, and for incongruities of all kinds. 'I don't know him well but I never really liked him, and I can't say this really surprises me,' he went on.

Roger said, taking a shot in the dark: 'He wouldn't be a member of the Lark Club, would he?'

There was a moment of surprised silence before Pengelly chuckled.

'I should have known you wouldn't take long to find that out. Yes, he is.'

'What do you know about Josiah Lark?'

Pengelly said slowly: 'I'm not sure. I don't think he's easy to know. But there are some background facts. He's a youngish man, trained in psychiatry, and he runs a free psychiatric clinic next door to the Lark Club. He's reputed to be wealthy and his club and clinic certainly seems to bear that out. I did a story on him for our Sunday supplement a few months ago.'

'That's where I'd heard of him,' Roger said. 'Ostensibly he's just a do-gooder, then.'

'Yes.'

'Do you mind if I tell him you told me about him?'

'I'd rather you didn't,' said Pengelly. 'He might resent it, and I prefer people to be friends.'

'Then I'll keep you out of it,' Roger promised. 'Thanks a lot, Pen.'

'Remember me if a story breaks, won't you?'

'I certainly will.'

'There have been two or three cases of acid throwing in the rougher districts, lately. Worth thinking about, isn't it?' Pengelly remarked.

'I'm thinking about it,' Roger said drily.

Pengelly rang off, and Roger lifted the internal telephone and dialled Chief Inspector Evans, who had a desk in one of the CI's rooms. Evans answered almost at once; next moment, Moriarty was on the line.

'I've traced Smith,' Roger announced. 'And I'm going over to the Lark Club, right away. Meet me at the foot of the main steps, will you?' He rang off, picked up his pencilled notes, and reminded himself of a primary rule of detection – follow one line of inquiry at a time. It was nearly six o'clock when he left his office. Moriarty was at the foot of the steps, by the side of his, Roger's, car.

'Like me to drive, sir?'

'Yes, please.'

Moriarty closed the door on Roger, took the wheel and moved off on to the Embankment, and then into a gap in the traffic. He did not say a word until Roger spoke, then volunteered the fact that he had talked to the Kensington Division about the Lark Club and knew as much about it as Roger, but:

'I'd no idea Smith – Osgood was a member.'

'One of the first things we need is a list of members,' Roger said. 'If Lark is co-operative that won't cause any trouble. We'll treat him very courteously, but show him the book of matches and Osgood's photograph.'

Moriarty said, almost fiercely: 'I'll be glad to watch you in action.'

He thought: And wait until you see *me* in action, Handsome!

They turned into Mountjoy Street, a narrow thoroughfare of tall terraced houses on the south side of Kensington Gardens, at Kensington Gore. There were a few private hotels, two houses for sale, three signs saying: *Furnished Flat To Let*, and, halfway down on the left hand side, four newly painted houses which put the rest of the terraces to shame. One was marked: *Psychiatric Clinic*, the other three were marked: *THE LARK CLUB*, with one word over each square portico. There was comfortable room for parking. Outside the clinic was a sign reading: *DOCTOR'S CAR*. In the space opposite was a silver grey Rolls Royce.

'All the signs of opulence,' Moriarty remarked.

'So I see,' Roger said thoughtfully.

An attractive, well-made-up girl opened the door. She wore a pale pink smock, cleverly cut; not quite a dress, not quite a uniform.

'Is Dr Lark expecting you?'

'No,' Roger said, 'we are—'

'Then I am afraid he can't possibly see you.' The interruption was smooth and practised. 'He has a number of evening appointments, and – oh!' The girl glanced down at Roger's card, and her expression and the tone of her voice changed. 'The *police*. What on earth—' she broke off.

'Just see if he can spare us ten minutes,' Roger said.

With obvious reluctance she stood aside for them to pass, then led them into a small but well-appointed waiting-room, and closed the door. The magazines on a beautifully carved sideboard were all up to date, the prints of old London on the wall were old, good, and beautifully framed. The paintwork was off-white, the wallpaper much the same colour.

They had been waiting for no more than three minutes when the door opened and a tall, striking-looking man came in. He had a hooked nose, a strong chin, and remarkably fine complexion. His knee length white coat was open to show a dark suit; he carried an evening paper in his hand.

He looked straight at Moriarty.

'Superintendent West?'

'I'm West,' Roger said. 'Nice of you to find time for us, sir.'

'When I saw *this* I expected a visit,' Lark said. He had a very clear, slightly high-pitched voice. He pointed to the photograph of 'John Smith' and went on: 'I'm afraid this is a most distressing reversion. The young man is a patient of mine – a voluntary patient who came to me acutely aware of his anti-social tendencies. I believed I was helping him and this revelation appals me. Nevertheless I am convinced it is only a temporary setback, and with the right treatment he will recover. However—' Lark was lecturing, obviously determined to get his say in first – 'it would be quite impossible for him to get the right treatment in *prison*, Superintendent. He should never have been remanded in custody. Is it possible to get that decision rescinded? Of course *I* will stand surety in any reasonable amount.'

CHAPTER NINE

MEMBERS' LIST

LARK, who had not moved during the monologue, hardly paused between sentences, maintaining his voice at a constant, slightly high-pitched level. He gave the impression that it did not occur to him that anyone could argue or disagree with him.

Roger said: 'That's a matter for the Court, sir.'

'Oh, come. The influence of the police—'

'Osgood is under the jurisdiction of the Court, not the police,' Roger said briskly. 'If you can satisfy the Court that remand in custody will be injurious to the man, I've no doubt they will try to help. How long has he been a patient?'

'For a year; a little more than a year.'

'When he came to you—'

'When he came to me he was a member of one of those pernicious East End gangs, Superintendent – it is a slur on our society that such gangs flourish, I cannot help feeling that if the police – ah – had more resources they would restrain such gangs. A friend who had been greatly helped brought him here. This relapse is most disappointing, but—'

'What kind of anti-social practice did this gang specialize in?' asked Roger.

'All kinds. Surely you don't need telling what they get up to, Superintendent. All kinds of crime from car-stealing and robbery to sexual offences—'

'Meaning what?'

'My dear Superintendent, do *you* need telling what a sexual offence is?'

Roger said: 'Such an offence can range from rape to assault, from comparatively trivial indecencies to homosexuality, sir. I am always interested when I hear of private treatment for such individuals. How many young men among your patients are perverts?'

'*Really*, Superintendent—'

'You don't think I should attempt to teach you your business, sir.'

'I do not.'

'And I think you might leave me to mine, and simply answer my questions,' Roger said coldly.

Lark drew back a pace, frowning. Roger noticed his surprisingly small and well-shaped hands, now raised in front of his chest. Suddenly, unexpectedly, he smiled, quite freely and naturally.

'You are very frank, Superintendent.'

'I hope you will be, too.'

'Except insofar as I must protect my patients' interests, I certainly will.'

'How many other patients have you with the same characteristics as Osgood?' Roger asked and added with a twinkle in his eyes: 'Or should I put it this way: are there any who haven't?'

'Oh, indeed, yes! Young people are not all sexually frustrated. In fact, a large proportion of my patients suffer not from such frustration but from the domination of their parents, or close friends, or even – particularly if they married young – husbands or wives. But of the hundred and seven clients whom I see regularly perhaps ten or twelve – no more than twelve – have the same characteristics, the same vulnerability to temptation.'

'*What* kind of temptation?'

'They have—' Lark hesitated, then frowned, raising his eyebrows so that his forehead became deeply furrowed. 'They *resent* any public, or semi-public, demonstrations of sexual love. A surprising number of young as well as middle-aged and elderly people find these demonstrations offensive. I can do little for the older age-groups, their ways are set, but the younger people – they have been influenced beyond doubt by over-demonstrativeness between their parents, at an early age. Young Osgood, for instance, lived in one room – one *room* – with his parents and two younger brothers, and – ah – was not always asleep when he was supposed to be. However – the chief reason, cause, fundamental basis of the sickness among my clients is an excessive degree of domination of one person by another. It can be, and often is, due to sexual influence or attraction and it can be due simply to the dominating and in some cases domineering influence of one personality over another. In criminal gangs – as you may well know, Superintendent – the leader usually dominates the others. He exerts his domination in the beginning by strength of character and the quality of leadership, but eventually he exercises it by *fear*. The victim is afraid to act on his own because (*a*) he loses self-confidence and (*b*) because the leader or other members of the gang frighten him into subservience or obedience.' Lark paused. 'I hope I do not appear to be usurping any function of the police, Superintendent, when I attempt to help young men who come under such influences.'

'Not in any way. Anything you or anyone else can do to break the dominance of gangs is very welcome.'

'Don't misunderstand me. Gang or group influence on sexual life is negligible. It is strong in other matters among certain people – the Germans, for example, under such a character as Hitler, the Russians under Stalin, the Egyptians under Nasser – these are significant demonstrations of political domination. But the domination of one person by another – parent, friend, lover, master – this is the cause of most of society's trouble and so, much of yours Superintendent. Because whenever a person so dominated seeks to break such domination he or she is liable to rebel against society and to commit a crime. So you see our activities – yours and mine – do overlap a great deal.'

'Yes,' Roger agreed with a lively smile, for he was enjoying this. 'Are any of these people familiar to you, Dr Lark?'

Moriarty handed over the photographs of last night's victims, fanned out like a card hand. Lark considered these one by one, shaking his head from time to time, until he reached the last – Anthony Wainwright. His expression changed, his lips tightened and he showed acute distaste.

'Wainwright,' he said. 'Was he the Wainwright involved in an unpleasant incident last night?'

'Yes.'

'I wish no human being harm or pain or even indignity, but that man deserves them all,' Lark stated icily.

'Why do you think that, sir?'

'He came here about a year ago, perhaps more than a year. He was introduced by a friend, and posed as a victim of his own irrepressible sexual and sadistic desires. It was not long before I discovered that he was seeing this as a *joke*. I heard him one evening telling club members that I had swallowed his story, hook, line, and sinker, as he put it. He exerted himself to break down the goodwill I had built up among patients who had become club members. He had in fact introduced other members who attempted to use the club as a – as a place of assignation. He is one of the most unpleasant persons I have ever met.'

Roger said: 'Someone else appears to have thought so.'

'Yes.'

'Do you know of anyone else with reason to hate him?'

'It is conceivable that he deeply distressed and antagonized other menbers of the club and other patients of mine.'

'May I have a list of your club members?'

'Certainly.'

'And of your patients.'

'Not in *any* circumstances,' answered Lark firmly. 'In no circumstances whatsoever.'

'Fair enough,' Roger said, and added almost as an aside: 'If we need to we can always get a Court order or a search warrant.' Moriarty made no comment, and Lark simply tightened his lips. 'What is the age group of your members, Dr Lark?'

'The maximum age is twenty-five.'

'And how do they apply and qualify for membership?'

'Usually by introduction, often because they come to me as a patient, and the club—' Lark broke off. 'I wish I had more time, I would very much like to show you over the club, but I have two patients to see and one of them is no doubt waiting for me already. I will gladly arrange for my club

65

manager to show you over the premises, if you wish.'

Roger said: 'I'd like that very much.'

'One moment, and I will see to it,' promised Lark. He turned and went out, moving very gracefully, and the door closed behind him.

Moriarty exuded a long, slow breath, and opened his lips to speak – but Roger gripped his arm and said very clearly:

'He obviously believes what he says.' He glanced about the room as he went on: 'The kind of man who might give us a lot of help if we could find a way of working together; we'll have to get to know him better.' He moved towards the big mirror, with the decorated corners, examining it closely as he went on: 'Don't you think so, Moriarty?'

'He's a very striking personality,' Moriarty said, clearly. Obviously he realized what Roger was doing and he moved to the prints. 'Now we know a little more about Wainwright, he seems to be a nasty piece of work.' Moriarty stopped – and pointed at one of the beautifully framed prints. Roger moved across and saw the tiny hole in it, cleverly concealed by the carving. There was no wire; this was almost certainly a minute tape-recorder. He nodded, and as they turned round the door opened again and Lark came in.

'Superintendent, I would like you both to meet Mr Delafield, who manages the Lark Club with very great efficiency. He will be happy to show you over the premises. . . . Hugh, this is Superintendent West and – ah—'

'Chief Inspector Moriarty,' Roger said.

'*Dela*field!' Moriarty echoed, as if incredulously.

They looked at a man a few years younger but uncannily like Albert Young in every feature. Only the expression was different; this man was relaxed in every way, smiling, pleasant, charming. If Moriarty's exclamation puzzled him he gave no sign as he shook hands.

'We are very proud of our club,' he said. 'I'll certainly be happy to show you round.'

The Lark Club, which could be approached from the street as well as from the Clinic, had been extensively converted from two Georgian houses. On the ground floor were the common rooms, for discussion, talks, television, reading – in every way it was like a traditional London Club except that the décor was more attractive, flowers abounded, and there were rather more women about than men. On the second floor were the 'private rooms', little more than cubicles with two armchairs in each, a telephone, a writing desk, a small radio, and a hot plate for simple cooking. The cubicles had folding doors which did not latch and the murmur of conversation came from several of them. On the top floor were the offices, as well-kept as the rest of the club. No one was up there, and Delafield opened a filing cabinet.

'I understand you would like a list of members.'

'Please,' Roger said.

'It *is* for police use only, isn't it?'

'Yes, of course.'

Delafield took out a folder, opened it and showed several typewritten sheets, all clipped together. He handed this to Roger, took off his glasses, and rubbed his eyes – eyes which were almost uncannily like Albert Young's.

'We had a list mislaid a week ago,' he said. 'I hesitate to say stolen, but – I'm a little nervous. Several of our members have ah – stopped coming, since the list disappeared. The young man Osgood is one of them. He—'

Delafield broke off and went tense.

From below, Roger heard a shout, what might have been a scream, and the thudding of feet rushing up the stairs. He swung round, but Moriarty beat him to the door and the head of the landing. They saw three youths on the landing below disappearing into the door which led to the cubicles, and almost immediately there were cries of alarm.

'My God!' gasped Delafied.

'Call—' began Roger urgently.

Moriarty literally leapt down the stairs, using the banister to steady himself, reached the lower landing and leapt down the flight below. Roger went swiftly but more cautiously, as the screaming began and the shouts and banging grew worse. As he reached the landing, two youths appeared, each wearing a nylon stocking stretched over his face. Each was carrying a spray gun, like a revolver in size and shape. At sight of Roger, they drew up.

'Drop those,' Roger said, sharply.

One of them muttered: 'Let him have it.'

Almost on the instant the spray guns were raised. Roger felt a flare of fear, heard the crying and the gasping and the moaning from the cubicles, then flung himself downwards, clutching at one man's ankle. He gripped and pulled, horribly aware of the overwhelming chance of acid spraying over the back of his head. He felt the other's leg yield, had a distorted view of the man crashing down on him.

Then he heard more footsteps, followed by Moriarty's voice.

'Don't *move*.' There was a pause. 'Don't *move* or *you'll* get some.'

Some what?

A sharp pain was slow burning now, and not very serious. Roger uncovered his face, and began to get to his knees. Moriarty was in the doorway, holding one of the spray guns. The man whom he, Roger, had brought down crouched on one knee, the other had disappeared. Someone was moaning, someone else was shouting: 'Get a doctor, a doctor.' Two men appeared from cubicles almost at the same time, one short and nearly bald, the other lanky and long haired. This man had a hand at his cheek.

Roger said: 'Wash all the wounds in cold water – that will help until the doctors come.' He turned his head. 'Mr Delafield, how soon can you get doctors here?'

'Some are on the way, sir,' said Moriarty. 'I sent a call—' he broke off, as a car squealed to a standstill outside the club. 'There are our men, now. The other two got away on motorcycles, but at least we've got this one.'

The man whom Roger had felled was on his feet, staggering. Was he going to make a desperate bid for escape, as Smith *alias* Osgood had done? He looked dazed and scared as he stared at the spray gun in Moriarty's hand. Moriarty's expression was set, as if he would use the gun at the slightest provocation.

Lark and the receptionist made their way through a huddle of terrified onlookers as three Divisional policemen mounted the stairs to the landing where Roger, Moriarty, and the prisoner were waiting.

'Take this man to Cannon Row,' Roger ordered. 'I'll see him there. And use the handcuffs – he may try to escape.' There was a bustle of movement and a sharp metallic click; for the first time Roger felt sure that the prisoner would not escape.

The police moved off with him as Lark came out of the cubicles.

The prisoner glared at Lark and said viciously: 'We'll get you, don't worry. You may think you're smart, but we'll get you.'

Then he allowed himself to be marched down the stairs, while the psychiatrist stared after him, looked at Roger, and asked:

'What on earth does he mean?'

'That's what I want to know,' Roger said. 'And I also want to know why they made this attack on your club members, sir.'

'I haven't the faintest idea,' declared Lark.

CHAPTER TEN

WELCOME HOME

'HE KNOWS,' Moriarty said, savagely.

'We can't be sure,' Roger said.

'He *must* know. It's some kind of feud.'

'It could be.'

'For God's sake don't be so cautious!' Moriarty cried.

They were sitting in Roger's car, heading for the Yard, an hour after the prisoner had been taken off. It was still broad daylight, and the evening air was humid and warm. A few men walked in shirt sleeves carrying their jackets. Behind them was a little stream of cars which Moriarty would not allow to pass.

Roger said coldly: 'I shall pretend I didn't hear that.'

Moriarty glanced at him, moistened his lips and muttered what might have been a grudging apology. Here was the evidence that he might quickly get too big for his boots. To talk back at a senior officer was as grave an offence at the Yard as in the armed services. He would probably regret it later, but his temper, on edge since he had snatched the spray gun, was always too hasty, and his self-control too liable to crack. For an awful moment Roger had feared that he would indeed use the acid on the prisoner.

Roger went on calmly: 'Yes, it might be some kind of feud.

Or it could be a deliberate attempt to involve Lark.'

'Er – in what way, sir?'

'By deliberately sending the raiders while we were there. Who knew where you were going?'

'No one.'

'Not even Evans?'

'*No* one, sir. I assumed you wouldn't want me to tell anyone else – without instructions.'

'You couldn't be more right. So, either we were seen approaching or entering, or Lark, his receptionist, or the man Delafield, could have sent word that we were there.'

Moriarty negotiated a zebra crossing, and then said: 'I don't quite understand, sir. You think someone told the acid throwers we were there and the raid was timed to coincide with our visit?'

'It could be.'

'What purpose would there be?'

'To make us believe that Lark's club is on the acid throwers' list.'

After another pause, Moriarty said: 'The receptionist or Delafield might have done that, but Lark wouldn't have.'

'Probably not,' Roger agreed. He half wished he hadn't said so much, for he was really thinking aloud, half-suggestions flitting through his mind. 'The other possibility is that the timing of the raid was sheer coincidence, but even then there would still have to be a motive. Does one spring to mind?'

Moriarty said: 'To close the club?'

'Yes. Or even to scare the wits out of Lark,' Roger suggested.

They were driving round Trafalgar Square in a stream of heavy traffic. The fountains were playing and a few youths, naked to the waist, were standing under the spray. A thin crowd of moving onlookers was on the far side, where the pigeons strutted in their hundreds, perched on shoulders, arms, and unwary heads, pecking at the corn sold by glib-tongued vendors. As they passed this spot and headed down Whitehall, Moriarty said very thoughtfully:

'Certainly we've been *forced* to consider Lark.'

'Which could be a good reason to consider it may be the wrong way to look,' Roger said.

They passed the Horse Guards, where dozens of sightseers

gathered to stare at two troopers of the Household Cavalry, seated like statues on unmoving horses.

'You certainly see every angle, don't you,' Moriarty said, and then in a very different tone, he went on: 'I always feel a bloody fool when I get mad. Please don't hold it against me, sir.'

They passed the Cenotaph, the memorial to millions who had died.

'We need results in this case,' Roger said, 'and we need them quickly and urgently. If we keep an eye on that ball, the rest isn't very important. And we need results—' he paused, as they slowed down to make the left turn into the Yard; ahead, Big Ben and the Houses of Parliament rose in stark sharpness against a pale blue sky from which the light was fading – 'because *they're* really beginning to know what a problem we've got with young people today.'

'They – oh! The politicians,' Moriarty sniffed.

'Our masters,' Roger reminded him.

He was glad when they came to a stop in the Yard, because he wasn't sure that Moriarty really understood what he was saying; he wasn't wholly sure that he understood himself. It had something to do with the fundamental importance of youth in tomorrow's world, a sense that it was not on the right road and that it was being led astray by such people as the young hooligans who sprayed acid. He realized that this was an instinctive belief which many at the Yard would deride, others simply not understand at all. Criminals were criminals, young or old, said one school of thought, and the evil doers had to be caught early and slapped down hard.

'I'll go over to Cannon Row and see the prisoner,' Roger said. 'If I need you I'll call – see what's new in my office, will you?'

'Right!' Moriarty, his brisk self again, spoke almost too quickly.

'Then take the spray gun and the acid up to the laboratory and ask them to test the acid, and check the gun,' Roger ordered. 'The quicker we get that done, the better.'

'I'll fix it, sir,' said Moriarty.

He thought: You're telling *me* to hurry. What a nerve!

*   *   *

Roger, quite unaware of Moriarty's true mood, went into the police station which was as familiar as the Yard itself. The night duty men were old acquaintances, old friends, and the Superintendent on duty was elderly, thoughtful, experienced, gruff. He was half a head taller and inches wider than Roger; a huge man.

'Got a rum 'un here, Handsome, haven't you?'

'This chap I sent over?'

'Yes. Won't give his name, won't say a word.'

'Record?' asked Roger.

'No. Just glares as if he hates the world,' the Superintendent said.

When he set eyes on the prisoner Roger knew exactly what the older man meant. The youth sat with his back against the wall, slouching, his hands limp in his lap. His hair was long and fell over his eyes; he looked through it, rather like a Cairn terrier. His lips were set in a sullen line, his whole body dropped.

'Have you had a go at him yourself?' Roger asked the Superintendent.

'I certainly have.'

No man was more likely to make a stubborn prisoner talk.

'Then we won't waste any more time,' Roger decided.

The duty sergeant opened the cell doors, keys clanging, and Roger was prepared for a sudden rush to escape, but none came. Instead, the prisoner's lips curled in a sneer, and he muttered:

'So you've got *some* sense.'

'Look, it can speak,' the Superintendent said with heavy humour.

Neither, however, could get another word out of the man.

Roger walked across to the Yard and up to his own office, where the light was on and Moriarty was sitting at a small table, several piles of the questionnaires in front of him. He jumped up.

'Any luck, sir?'

'None, I'm afraid. What do you make of those?'

'The final one you approved seems just right,' said Moriarty.

'Get copies done first thing in the morning, and send plenty round to each Division,' Roger said. 'Make it your first job – if anything crops up to stop you, telelphone me at home.'

'Right, sir!' Moriarty pushed his chair away. 'Can I drop you?'

'Good idea,' Roger said, appreciatively.

Twenty minutes later they slowed down to turn into Bell Street. On the far side was a group of youngsters of both sexes and among them Roger caught a glimpse of Richard's alert face. Richard spotted him, too, and pointed. A fair-haired, pleasant-looking girl was holding his arm. Then Martin showed up. Roger glanced round as he got out of the car; the group was coming towards him.

'Now if they were in twos—' Moriarty began, but stopped abruptly.

'I know what you mean,' Roger said. 'My sons are there.'

'*Are* they, then.' Moriarty was closing the door. 'Like them tagged, sir?'

'I'll see,' said Roger.

He waited at the gate, knowing that Richard in particular liked to introduce him to friends who might be impressed by a senior Yard officer, a harmless vanity which could be humoured. All six of them were hurrying. Roger heard them talking – then heard a rustle of movement in the privet hedge and spun round, seeing a man with a spray gun in his mind's eye. There was a cat, crouching.

Richard drew up first.

'Hallo, Dad! This is Elsie Jones, she wants to say hallo! Elsie, this is my father.'

'Hallo, Elsie.' She was tall, fair, nice-looking, and Roger took to her.

'I didn't really believe Richard when he said you were *the* Superintendent West.' The girl's hand was cool, her speech was rather hurried; breathless. 'Whatever Richard says, *I* think you're wonderful, Mr West.'

Martin's deep voice followed, a chuckle in it.

'Now you know what Fish thinks of you, Pop!'

'Oh, I didn't mean to say—' began Elsie in alarm.

'Charlotte would like to say hallo, too,' Martin went on as a little dark-haired girl came forward, much more timidly.

'Hallo, Charlotte!' Roger welcomed her.

'Hi,' she said, and held his hand longer than he had expected. 'Tell him, Martin.'

'No, don't be silly.'

'Then I shall.'

'Oh, we'd better tell him or she'll keep on making a fuss,' Richard said, in exasperation. 'We were followed by three louts, Dad – thought they were going to start a fight at one time. The girls were quite scared.'

Roger felt himself go cold.

'Where was this?' he asked quietly.

'Walking across Eelbrook Common, twenty minutes ago. If the other two hadn't come along, I think they might have jumped us,' Richard went on.

'We were just walking,' Charlotte said airily in delicate explanation.

'Holding hands,' Elsie amended.

'We'd soon have fixed *them*,' declared Richard.

'He wanted to turn and go for them,' remarked Scoop, the chuckle deeper in his voice. 'Fat lot of use that would have been if they'd squirted acid over us.'

Roger, still feeling icy cold, said: 'Don't take chances, Fish. How far have these girls to go home?' He noticed that the other couple had already crossed the street.

'Oh, only round the corner,' Elsie said. 'Mr – Superintendent, I mean!'

'Yes?'

'There *is* danger then?'

The only possible answer was: 'Yes, there could be,' and it would be folly to say anything else. Yet Roger did not answer at once, for it suddenly dawned on him that what these young people were half afraid of, now, might affect *all* young couples. It dawned on him that the attacks in Chelsea and Shepherd's Bush, although without acid, had done a great deal more damage than he had realized. It was not simply that couples who were using the cover of darkness for their love-making might be attacked; any young couples might be. 'We were just walking.' Or were holding hands; or kissing.

'Of course there's no *danger*!' Richard scoffed.

'There's enough risk not to take any chances at all,' Roger warned him.

'*Now* we'll have to behave ourselves,' murmured Martin.

'You don't think it's a deep laid plot by antediluvian parents, do you?' asked Charlotte. She had a wicked smile. 'I thought my father looked at me rather forbiddingly this evening when he asked me who I was going out with.'

'I think it's more likely a deep laid plot by one gang against members of another,' Roger said. 'But we don't know how many people are involved, and a lot of silly young idiots might start fooling about. Like me to see you all home, Fish?'

'Come on!' Richard grabbed Elsie and raced her away. They were all laughing as the other youngsters hurried off. Roger watched them, smiled, and then turned towards the front door, yet as he took out his key, he hesitated. 'I suppose they *will* be all right,' he asked himself in a low-pitched voice, then braced himself and went on more loudly: 'Of course they will!'

The door opened as he spoke, and Janet stood there.

He was reminded vividly of the way Albert Young had appeared in his front door, last night; as vividly of Janet's touchiness yesterday, her sensitivity to the job he was doing, and her distaste. In the instant while the two thoughts flashed through his mind he wondered how much Janet had overheard, and what her mood would be like because of it. Then suddenly her arms were about him and she hugged him with a vigour and warmth of feeling she hadn't shown in months.

'Hallo, darling!'

'Hallo. What have I done right?'

'I was afraid you'd be late,' she said and they slipped into an arms-round-each-other's-waist position, as Roger closed the door with his foot. 'Hungry?'

'Famished!'

'I've a casserole hot,' Janet said. She looked young and almost gay, her eyes bright, her hair fluffed and attractive. 'Darling,' she went on, 'I'm sorry I was a pig yesterday, I don't know what got into me. You're quite a hero in the Bridge Club for tackling the job, and the things some of them said about their children made me realize how lucky we are with ours.' They entered the brightly lit but slightly shabby kitchen. 'Everyone's talking about it. Somehow it's made all the smug and self-satisfied parents realize that the young *are* a problem today and it's no use saying it was the same when they were young. This age is different, somehow – there seems more danger for them. This beastly business makes it more obvious, that's all.' She let him go, and moved to the oven door; then

75

she turned to face him and he read the anxiety, even the fear, in her eyes. 'Our two *are* all right, aren't they? No one will attack them?'

She was really saying: 'No one will attack them because you're you, will they?'

CHAPTER ELEVEN

WIDER IMPLICATIONS

ROGER put an arm round Janet's still slender waist, and kissed the tip of her nose. He didn't answer immediately; whatever else, his answer mustn't be glib, had to be truly considered.

He said at last: 'They're on the look-out, and so am I. There's been at least one attack on me personally.'

'Roger!'

'I don't mean bodily assault. I mean that photograph.'

Her alarm faded.

'... and yes, these brutes could have a go at the boys. Did you hear what was said outside?'

Janet coloured a little.

'Yes, I – er – I was at the bedroom window.'

'So you know they think they were followed. Jan, they're *men* now.'

'Men! They're children!'

'Men within most meanings of the word,' Roger said. 'Old enough to fight, be married, have children, get girls into trouble, get into trouble themselves. We don't have to fool ourselves, do we?'

Janet was frowning, her eyes very thoughtful and shadowed.

'I suppose not.' She pressed his wrists and turned away, took out the casserole and placed it on the table; only one place was laid. As Roger washed at the sink, the back door opened and Richard whistled: '*Phwee-phwoo*,' and the boys came in, bright-eyed, boisterous. Richard sniffed ostentatiously.

'Smells good.'

'You've had yours!'

'I'm still allowed to *smell* your good cooking, aren't I?'

Janet said resignedly: 'I ought to have had more sense than

to think there would be enough for tomorrow. Get out a knife and fork.'

Soon they were all eating, all, that is, except Janet who sat without a plate in front of her. Sitting there, she looked younger than her years – too young to be the mother of two such hefty sons. It was Martin who looked up at his father with a half-laughing, half-serious grin and remarked:

'They've given you a tough job this time, Dad, haven't they?'

'Which one, in particular?'

'Guarding the morals of the youth of the day.'

Roger looked at him levelly and said: 'Have they any?'

'Proper old cynic, our father,' observed Richard. 'Elsie thought you were *dreamy*.'

'Are we talking about morals, general, or morals – specific, sexual?' inquired Martin professionally.

'Scoop!' protested Janet.

Her elder son looked at her. 'I wonder why women, really the sexier sex, always pretend to be shocked when it's talked about? Don't you think that's why it's acquired a certain nastiness, an *indecency*?'

Janet looked at him steadily for a long time, and he returned her gaze without embarrassment, until there was a curious tension in the homely kitchen, all the lightness and brightness slowly seeping out of the atmosphere. Roger thought: I don't want to have to take sides in this. He said lightly: 'Morality is such a wide subject, ranging from ethics to a mere code of behaviour. What did you mean, Scoop, when you said my job was guarding the morals of the youth of the day?'

Martin-called-Scoop coloured very slightly.

'I was being a bit facetious, I suppose.'

'Well, now be serious.'

'It *is* quite a job you've taken on, isn't it?' Richard said.

'It's quite a job I've been given, but I don't think that's what Scoop was driving at.'

'No, it wasn't, really,' Martin agreed. 'I was thinking as we walked home tonight and those chaps followed us, there must be hundreds of thousands of couples out on their own this evening, and if they've read the evening papers most of them must have wondered if *they* would be attacked. A lot of girls are nervous of a kiss and cuddle in the woods—' he shot a

77

"sorry mum" glance at Janet – 'and after this I'll bet a lot of chaps have been disappointed.'

'And you can't even be safe walking along the street,' Richard weighed in. 'She didn't let you see it, Dad, but Elsie was really frightened.'

'It was excuse enough to need your protective arm,' Martin observed drily. 'So when you look at it straight, Dad, *you're* really fighting for the right of young couples to cuddle undisturbed!'

'They're not *men*,' Janet said helplessly. 'They're ogres. There's some jam tart in the larder.'

'I'll get it.' Richard leapt to his feet.

Roger said thoughtfully: 'The police are trying to do what they always do, Scoop – protect the people from any infringement of their rights and liberties, We're not concerned as policemen with what you ought to do, with the rights or wrongs of social behaviour – we just try to make sure the rules are observed.'

Richard slapped a small piece of jam tart and two cartons of yoghourt on the table.

'What are the chances over this case?' he inquired.

'*Who ate that tart?*' demanded Janet in outraged protest.

'I had a bit,' confessed Martin after a pause.

'A bit!'

'So did I,' confessed Richard. 'It was jolly good. Well, Dad?'

Roger said: 'I don't want any, Jan, thanks. On the whole the chances of solving this case easily are not so good,' he added to Richard. 'We don't yet know the motive, and that's always a handicap. If someone wants to throw a scare into young folk, this is a pretty good way of doing it. And that could be the answer.'

'Burning their backsides with acid is pretty drastic,' Martin remarked drily.

'I wish it were only their backsides! Yes, it's drastic, cruel and sadistic, and I hope it's not the answer,' Roger said. 'I'd much rather find that the victims of the acid-spraying are specific individuals attacked with a personal motive, and that the lesser attacks are either imitative or made to heighten the effect. Don't worry too much, Scoop, I've got a lot of help on the job, but you and Richard want to keep your eyes *very* wide open. There's enough evidence to show that the criminals might turn this into a feud against me – they may even be trying to throw a scare into me and the Yard, for some obscure reason. Nothing's better calculated to frighten than acid in the face,' he added almost casually. 'Obviously they might decide I'd lose my nerve quicker if I thought you two might be in danger.'

'Our behaviour, for the period of the emergency, will be impeccable,' Martin promised. 'May I stay home and help you, Mother?'

Janet only half-laughed.

'It's *not* funny,' she protested.

Martin gave his broadest grin.

'It is, some of the time,' he said.

It was after one o'clock before they all got to bed. Roger wondered uneasily whether there would be any reports of more trouble that night, but at least nothing had happened, so far, to make it worth calling him.

Moriarty tapped lightly on the door of Helena Young's room, which was beneath his own, but there was no answer. Presumably she was asleep. He went upstairs and opened his briefcase, then began to type notes and reports. It was half past two before he went to bed.

It was twenty to seven when he woke, and one of his first thoughts was: I wonder how much of West's job I'll have to do for him today.

Roger turned into his office at a quarter to nine that morning and found a sheaf of typewritten reports, with a note on top saying: 'No significant developments during the night. Jill Hickersley (the Chelsea girl) is round from the sedation.' Roger skimmed through the reports and then called an elderly Superintendent who had become an efficient – but unadmitted – office manager. Roger talked . . .

'How long is this Moriarty going to be here?' the other inquired.

'I'd guess, from four to five weeks, unless he's transferred permanently.'

'No reason why you shouldn't put him in Room 27, then,' said the older man. 'It's been empty since the last big door-to-

79

door inquiry. It's got a desk, a typewriter, phones – the lot.'

'Thanks,' said Roger. He rang off, and called Moriarty.

'I'll be right along, sir.'

As Roger's door opened, he was half-prepared for the alertness, the freshness, the sense of controlled vitality in Moriarty, and he had a flash almost of jealousy for the days when he himself had approached every morning with the same aggressive determination to make this the *day*.

'Good morning, sir.'

''Morning. Sit down.'

'Thank you.'

'What do you mean by "no significant developments"?' Roger demanded.

'There were three attacks on couples last night, no acid, nothing at all to connect them with the main case, sir. Two youths were caught – they really *were* larking about. The third was a jealous husband.' Roger nodded. 'Helena Young had a good night – she was still asleep when I left. Wainwright, no change. Neither of the prisoners has said another word. Jill Hickersley's still in a state of shock but she's named the man who was with her.'

'Ah!'

'A Clive Davidson – who's staying at the YMCA in Tottenham Court Road, according to her.'

'Isn't he?' asked Roger.

'He has a room there sometimes, but hasn't been in for several days,' Moriarty answered. 'No luggage.'

'A man of mystery, this Clive Davidson,' Roger mused. 'Why do you think he ran?'

'Anyone's guess, sir. Mine—' he hesitated.

'Go on.'

'If he were a married man and didn't want his wife to know about his *amours*, he would have good reason to run.'

'Got a call out for him?' asked Roger.

'Yes, sir. But the girl hasn't a photograph.'

'How long's she known him?'

'About a month. She shares a flat with an older girl, a Daisy Hill, but Daisy's away this week.'

'Parents? Relations?'

'She's on her own – says her parents are dead. She works in an antique shop in the Fulham Road, a sales assistant.'

'Do you know how she met this Clive Davidson?'

'At a party, I gathered, but she's very vague,' Moriarty said. 'I thought I'd go and have a word with her myself today, sir.'

'Do that. Is there anything from Lark?' Roger changed the subject without a change of tone.

'Several of the club members were badly marked with pretty nasty burns. Nothing which plastic surgery won't put right, but it'll be a long business. There's anxiety about a man with cardiac trouble, that's the most serious.'

'Have we anything more on Lark?'

'Not exactly,' Moriarty said.

'What does that mean?' Roger wanted to know.

'There's a bit of a mystery about where he came from and where he got his money,' Moriarty told him. 'He's a bachelor, but—' there was a long pause.

'Go on.'

'Quite a man for the ladies.'

'*Club* members?'

'As a matter of fact, sir,' said Moriarty, 'I think we ought to have a man in that club. From what I can gather it's not difficult to become a patient and not difficult to become a member if you're a patient. We could use someone who looks young enough to pass—'

Roger grinned. 'Such as Moriarty!'

'I'm known there, sir, I wouldn't be any use,' Moriarty said evenly.

'I'll think about it,' Roger promised. 'We want to find out how many first offenders Lark treats and how many, if any, are members of the club,' he went on. 'Make sure that's started at once.'

'It's already started, sir.'

'Oh.' Moriarty was very determined to show how good he was, and almost cocky with it. The time would come, Roger suspected, when he would have trouble with Moriarty; there was something in the younger man's manner that he disliked, almost mistrusted; but this was not the time to force an issue. Those questionnaires are being distributed, I take it?'

'They've gone, sir.'

'Good,' Roger said, with forced heartiness. 'I've arranged for you to work in Room 27 while we're on this job; get what tables you need for keeping the questionnaire replies sorted and tabulated. You might get the Map Room Inspector to prepare some kind of graph so that we can keep a daily check – and you'll need some maps – four, each showing a quarter of the Metropolitan Police District, I would say. All clear?'

'Clear and understood, sir.'

Roger nodded dismissal but Moriarty wasn't ready to go.

'One other thing, sir.'

'What's that?'

'The newspapers are going to town on this, you know.'

'You'd expect them to, wouldn't you?'

'Some are pretty circumspect, some very blunt,' Moriarty went on as if there'd been no interruption. 'I was thinking—' he paused, long enough for Roger to prompt:

'Yes?'

'This is going to have a very disheartening effect on courting couples.'

'Yes, I daresay it is.'

'There may be fewer around,' Moriarty went on.

Roger said drily: 'It wouldn't surprise me.' He half-expected Moriarty to come up with the suggestion that this might be the motive, a kind of 'purification by burning' but instead Moriarty said:

'We could put up a few stooges, couldn't we? Get a couple of our younger officers of both sexes to wander about the commons and parks. If they were attacked, we could have a few more prisoners and they can't all go dumb on us.'

Roger stared at him, his mind working very fast; and then he laughed.

'Might be a good idea but I'd need authority before we did it, and we'd probably be wise to call for volunteers. I'll think about that, too.' As Moriarty went to the door, Roger added: 'Keep all of this under your hat. We don't want any leakages.'

'*Absolutely* confidential,' Moriarty assured him, and went out.

When the door closed, with a curious deliberation, Roger asked himself: 'What *is* there about him I don't like?'

'I'll think about it – *think* about it. And he's supposed to be famous for getting a move on,' Moriarty muttered. 'Doesn't he *want* results?'

CHAPTER TWELVE

ACID TEST

ROGER WENT upstairs to the laboratory, after Moriarty had gone, and saw a middle-aged man with a pink bald head and a pink double chin in a khaki smock that was a little too tight for him. On the bench nearby was the spray gun and next to it a small bottle filled with a colourless liquid. Other younger men were at different parts of the bench, Bunsen burners and crucibles, pipettes and microscopes were all in use.

The double-chinned man said: 'Didn't think it would be long before you turned up.'

'I've got to pressure you for results somehow,' Roger joked.

'All you ever think of – pressuring. Scientific investigation takes time, my boy. You might tell your impetuous young friend that.'

Roger said sharply: 'Moriarty? Has he been here?'

'Once last night and twice this morning. He seems to think we can identify odourless acid by sense of smell.'

'How have you identified it?' Roger asked.

'By chemical analysis,' answered the other. 'It's simple concentrated sulphuric acid all right; it should have been made more difficult to get years ago. Too many kids kill themselves with it. The spray is an ordinary insecticidal spray for liquids, made of polyethylene, used for powders as well as liquids, and a good quality one – nothing leaks. It's filled by dipping it into a container of the acid – you can see where the paint's been burned off,' he pointed. 'The users must always wear special gloves or take a chance of burning their fingers pretty badly. I know I'm teaching my grandma to suck eggs, but this stuff's cool as a dove when it settles on the skin, but if it isn't washed off in a few seconds, it begins to burn – and believe me, it burns deep. Dehydrates the flesh, as it were.'

Roger nodded.

'Can you distinguish one manufacturer's product from another?'

'The only guide is the strength. This is ninety per cent pure, and I only know one firm which makes it – most English manufacturers use eighty-four or eighty-five per cent.'

83

'What's the firm?' asked Roger.

'An old and reputable one – Webb, Son, and King, over at Wandsworth, near the river. Has to be by a river for this kind of job – they use a lot of water and disgorge a lot of waste. Know what concentrated sulphuric acid is used for, don't you?'

'Cleaning and what they call pickling,' Roger hazarded.

'And it's used a lot to make ammonium sulphate, the fertilizer crystals. Use it in the manufacture of dyes, too, but Webb, Son, and King will tell you a lot more than I can. The sprays are a brand called Amo, they can be bought at any gardener's supply stores or agricultural instrument makers, or any nurseryman's store. Like all this written down?'

Roger grinned.

'Yes, please!'

'Can't do a report until tomorrow, Handsome, not even for you.'

'That's all right,' Roger said. 'Can you send the spray gun down to Fingerprints?'

'Why not take it yourself – not that you'll find anything much. Plastic gloves must have been used, very risky to touch that with the bare hands.'

'Lend me a pair of the gloves,' Roger said.

He went downstairs to a small room in which a bench was heaped with all kinds of bottles, boxes, sticks, knives, suit-cases, drawers, every conceivable object one might find in a junk shop. Those on the desk were exhibits waiting to be finger-printed, those on the floor were waiting, reports attached, to be taken away. The Inspector in charge of Finger-prints was tall and melancholy.

'No,' he said.

'You never could,' retorted Roger. 'Just do me a spot check on one small spray gun, Barney.'

Barney said: 'Acid spray?'

'Yes.'

'I've got a daughter,' Barney remarked. 'Gimme.' He took the spray gun with great caution and moved it towards a window above the bench. In front of him were a dozen different kinds of powder, camel hair brushes, and all the impedimenta of his trade, as well as three Contraflex cameras with which to get instant prints. Now he used a grey powder and brushed it

84

carefully over the surface, then donned a pair of powerful-looking glasses.

'One set,' he said, 'superimposed over a lot of smears.'

The smears would be the prisoner's; the prints, Moriarty's, Roger reflected.

'Sure there's only one set?'

'See for yourself,' proffered Barney. 'There's the thumb – the fingers – and the palm on the knob of the handle. Like some photographs?'

'Please,' said Roger. 'Thanks a lot, Barney.'

'Don't think I did it for you – just for the Youth of the Space Age. Having any luck?' Barney was obviously hopeful.

'Could be.'

'Keep smiling,' Barney said.

Roger went out, and as he turned towards the lift a girl came towards him, wearing a light green cotton dress. She was a pleasant looking girl, and her fair hair reminded him of Richard's Elsie.

'Good morning, sir.'

Roger said: 'Good morning.' They passed, and then he stopped and turned. 'Detective Constable Reed, aren't you?'

She turned, too; she moved very easily, in a naturally provocative way.

'Yes, sir.'

'What job have you been out on?'

'Decoy for nasty old men,' she answered. 'As a matter of fact, sir, I have to change into uniform and go and give evidence.'

'Any job assigned after that?' asked Roger thoughtfully.

The girl said slowly: 'Well, no, sir.'

'Do you know what I'm working on?'

'Of course, sir.'

Very deliberately, Roger said: 'You've an exceptionally nice complexion.'

As deliberately, Detective Constable Hilary Reed said: 'If I used a special matt make-up, sulphuric acid wouldn't do much harm, sir. I'd have time to wipe it off.'

Roger smiled, broadly.

'In that case I may have a job for you.'

'Thank you, sir. I'll look forward to it.'

Roger went downstairs and along to the office of Chief

85

Inspector in charge of the women Criminal Investigation Officers. He knew her well; she had been transferred to the Yard from the same Division as he, fifteen years ago. Those who did not know her thought her aloof and cold-blooded. Roger remembered her saying once: 'What urges me or any woman to take up police work I shall never know. It compels us to mix with humanity at its absolute filthiest. I never let any girl join without trying to frighten her off.'

'Roger, I'd love to spend half an hour on your problem,' she said, 'but I've a conference in five minutes.'

'Can I use Detective Constable Reed for an inside job?' Roger asked. 'At the Lark Club?'

'Must you?'

'Can you think of anyone better?'

'No,' admitted the older woman, rather reluctantly. 'I'll arrange it. She'll report to you when she's finished in court.'

'Thanks,' Roger said. 'And she doesn't need any more warning how nasty this job could be.'

He left almost immediately, went back to his office, and found several drafts of proposed general calls on his desk, each from Moriarty. Moriarty wanted all London Divisions and Home Counties Police to look for Clive Davidson, and there was a brief description of the man. He also wanted a photograph of the prisoner who would not give his name circulated to Divisions, all police forces, all newspapers and television authorities. The 'calls' were precisely typed and well-spaced as well as effectively worded. Moriarty was showing him, Roger, how to do his job, of course; tolerance and patience were obviously needed. Roger rang for him, and he arrived with the promptitude of a genie summoned by the rubbing of Aladdin's lamp.

'Yes, sir?'

'Where'd you get the description of Davidson from?'

'The YMCA staff, sir.'

'The Hickersley girl's would be better. Has she seen it?'

'No, I doubt if she's—'

'I'll take it over to the hospital and see her,' Roger said. 'And before we spread the prisoner's photograph around I want to see what happens in court this morning.'

'Can that make any difference?' demanded Moriarty impatiently.

Roger said: 'It could. So could thinking before acting. If we broadcast and telecast his photograph, we virtually tell his friends that we don't know who he is. If we don't tell them, they may think he's talked.' He allowed that to sink in, wondering whether Moriarty was as disapproving as he seemed to be, and went on: 'I'm going to send a woman "patient" to Lark – Detective Constable Reed. I'll brief her this afternoon, and you'd better sit in.'

Moriarty's eyes glowed.

'That way you'll be able to find out if Lark's the lad he's supposed to be with women.'

'That's right,' said Roger.

'Damn good!' enthused Moriarty.

Roger just checked himself from saying sarcastically that he was glad Moriarty approved.

'I've had a report in about those first offenders Lark's helped – treated, rather,' Moriarty went on. 'Seven altogether - just kids who went astray I should say.'

'Keep checking,' Roger ordered.

'Keep checking, keep checking – why doesn't he worry about the *real* problems,' Moriarty muttered to himself. 'Why doesn't he find this man Davidson, and *make* Wainwright talk?'

Roger had hardly been in his office for five minutes when the telephone bell rang. He answered with his usual briskness.

'Jackson of Brixton here,' a man said, and Roger had an immediate mind picture of a melancholy-looking doctor at Brixton Prison. 'Your man Osgood's cracking. Do you want to see him?'

'I'll be right over,' Roger promised eagerly.

He was at Brixton within twenty minutes, and saw that Osgood was in a state of near collapse. Dr Jackson was looking at him sadly, and Roger's heart dropped.

'He didn't say anything worthwhile,' Jackson said. '*You* try.'

'I can't say any more, you should know that. I simply can't!' Osgood babbled. 'If I say anything my mother will get sprayed, if anyone talks that always happens – someone gets sprayed! I can't say anything else, for God's sake don't make me!'

'We could protect—' Roger began.

'No one can protect her! If they say they'll use the spray, they do it. I tell you they do it!'

"They" certainly struck terror into this youth, and Roger remembered vividly how Pengelly had reminded him that, of late, there had been a number of acid-spraying cases thought to be acts of reprisal. If that were so, it meant that the use of the acid as a terror weapon was being carefully calculated.

Could it be by a gang of fanatics? Wasn't it much more likely that there was a powerful material motive, as yet unsuspected?

Roger had to drop the thought into the back of his mind as he left Brixton. If he pushed his questions further, obviously he would drive Osgood out of his mind, whereas Jackson would work on him slowly and skilfully. Meanwhile, Osgood's mother would be watched closely. He gave instructions for this over the radio, and went on to see Jill Hickersley.

He liked her heart-shaped face, her big eyes, her fringe of dark hair, even her sense of outraged modesty. She was less distracted than Moriarty had led him to believe, and when Roger arrived a big, floppy girl was sitting with her – her flatmate, Daisy.

'I should *never* have left you,' Daisy was saying. 'I won't ever again, I promise you.' She seemed to tell West to put *that* in his pipe and smoke it, before she flounced out. Roger hitched up a chair and asked Jill to read the call for Davidson Jill frowned as she read it, then put it down.

'I wish I knew why he ran away. Mr West, do *you* think he was married?'

'I can't afford to guess,' Roger said, and thought: he may have been frightened out of his wits, like Osgood.

'Daisy can,' the girl said with a sigh.

'Is that description accurate?'

'Well – not very,' she said. 'It makes him seem so old.'

'Old?'

'Yes – he acted as if he were but he wasn't much older than I am – twenty-one,' she added naively.

'If I send an artist over to you with an Identi-kit outfit, will you help him to get a likeness of Clive Davidson for identification purposes?'

She hesitated.

'Why don't you want to?' Roger asked gently.

She said slowly and unhappily: 'It's not as if he'd done anything, is it? I mean, committed a crime you want to arrest him for. He may *be* married, and if his picture is in the newspapers and on television his wife is sure to see it. And that's bound to cause her a lot of distress.' Jill hitched herself up on her pillows, so that she could look at him more straightly and went on: 'I don't like refusing to help the police but *is* this so very important?'

After a pause, Roger answered: 'It might be very important indeed. Will you help with the picture and trust me not to use it unless I think it's essential?'

Her face cleared instantly.

'Of course!'

As he left the hospital, Roger thought almost light-heartedly: Who's saying the youngsters are all bad?

He made the arrangements for the Identi-kit picture but left instructions not to use it without express permission, told Moriarty, and felt that they were making some progress. Later in the afternoon, he briefed Detective Constable Hilary Reed about her assignment with Josiah Lark.

Detective Constable Hilary Reed was several years older than she looked; it was easy for her to pose as a girl of twenty-one. She made an appointment with Lark by telephone, and reached the clinic, wearing a slim fitting twin set, cut rather low in the neck, a little after five o'clock. Everything was normal except for two uniformed policemen and the two plainclothes men in a car within sight of the house – the protection Lark had asked for. She was shown into the waiting-room where Roger and Moriarty had been, and kicked her heels for twenty minutes. All she heard were people passing and cars moving along the street.

Then the door opened, admitting the receptionist, whose cool voice informed her that Dr Lark would see her now.

Hilary followed the girl into a large room, furnished more like an office than a surgery or consulting room, with a long, opulent-looking couch placed on one side but not flush with the wall. Lark, in his white smock, did not stand up from his desk, but waved to a chair.

'Sit down, Miss Reed ... That's right ... I understand you

were recommended by a friend ... Miss who? ... Hewson, oh yes, I remember ... Yes ... Now I want you to be absolutely at ease, Miss Reed ... Do you *feel* relaxed? ... Ah, a little tense, that is understandable and honest, a pleasing start ... Not all of my patients *are* honest, they seem to think it part of a psychiatrist's stock-in-trade to know when they are being lied to, and it isn't ... You could, if you wished, deceive me completely.'

Hilary Reed thought: It's almost as if he knows who I am.

'And there can be no good from this consultation or any other consultation unless you are completely frank,' went on Lark. 'Unless you tell me as lucidly as you can what goes on in your mind and why you are worried.' He glanced down at a card in front of him. 'I see that you told my receptionist that you are troubled by sexual fantasies and – ah – a sense of being imprisoned ... A welcome frankness again, so few people admit freely that they have such fantasies ... Do you live alone, Miss Reed?'

'No. With my mother,' Hilary answered.

'In a flat? Rooms? A house?'

'In a flat in St John's Wood.'

'So you are – reasonably well-provided for.'

'Yes. I've enough to live comfortably.'

'What work do you do?'

'Mostly voluntary and charity work,' Hilary answered. 'I think the truth is that I don't have enough to do.'

'Possibly,' said Lark, 'Yes, possibly. I – oh, excuse me.'

He broke off as the telephone bell rang, leaned across and picked up the instrument, staring up at the ceiling as if he had become suddenly oblivious of her. At first she thought this was an act. Then suddenly his expression changed and his lips tightened to a thin line; he looked afraid. He glanced at Hilary Reed, then said harshly:

'Hold on.' He put his hand over the mouthpiece and said: 'Excuse me, Miss Reed. Be good enough to wait outside.'

As she reached the door she heard him say in strangled, almost horrified tones:

'Oh, *no*!'

CHAPTER THIRTEEN

OPEN DOOR

HILARY REED stepped outside the door, closed it with a sharp click, opened it again on the instant, and stood there with her fingers on the handle, listening and looking about her. She was on the first floor landing, a mahogany staircase, darkly lustrous, stretching above and below her, A wide passage ran in either direction, with two doors leading from it. The receptionist was downstairs but there was no telling who might come out of these doors.

'. . . *no*,' breathed Lark again.

There was another silence. A door opened below, and Hilary was ready to move. Footsteps were muffled by a carpet but the street door was opened, and the receptionist said in her cool, impersonal voice:

'Good evening, Mr Laidlaw, please come in . . . Dr Lark won't keep you long.'

Now Lark was speaking again and the movements and noise below made it hard to hear what he was saying.

'. . . dreadful, I didn't think . . . Yes, of course we must be very careful indeed or we shall spoil everything . . . But we cannot throw away all we have done, it would be such a waste . . . Yes, I will see you later . . . Dreadful, quite dreadful. I'm shocked. Deeply shocked.'

There was a ting! as the receiver went down.

Hilary moved away, repeating to herself all he had said over and over again, reached a window overlooking the back of the house and saw a tall conservatory, the glass roof lined with big leaves of exotic plants; green, purple, red, even blue-tinged. She opened her bag, took out a diary, and noted the words which Lark had uttered, in shorthand. There was no sound now. She looked about, wondering how long Lark would keep her, whether, indeed, he would finish the interview. What *were* those plants? Castor oil – rubber – these were certainly among them. From this tall window it was like looking down on a jungle from an aeroplane. She shifted her position, her eye caught by a profusion of vivid yellow flowers. Beyond them was another conservatory filled with orchids in great variety.

There was no warning sound, just Lark's voice, close behind her. She started violently.

'Admiring my plants, Miss Reed?'

'Yes. Yes, they're remarkable,' she said, recovering quickly.

'Not beautiful?' He gave the impression that he was thinking about something else.

'Some of them are.'

'Yes, indeed. You are yourself a very attractive young woman, Miss Reed.'

Here it came.

'How kind of you to say so.'

'Truth *is* the truth. One of the things I am constantly trying to instil into my patients is the need for truth – above all, truth about oneself. You are, for instance – and you have admitted that you are – lonely.'

'My mother—' Hilary began.

'A comfort, at times. A burden and a liability at others. You need the company of younger people and of the opposite sex.'

'I – I suppose I do.' She stood with her back to the conservatory, looking straight into his face. The skin was smooth textured and in its way exceptional. There was a delicacy, a refinement about his features which had an almost feminine appeal. His nostrils were curved and very slightly distended, his mouth was well-shaped but rather small.

'As you must have gathered I have had some most distressing news,' Lark said.

'I'm sorry.'

'One of my patients – and a club member here – has died.'

'Oh, I am sorry.' What *did* one say?

'As a result of a dastardly attack made here last night – are you aware of what happened, Miss Reed?'

'Wasn't it – in the newspapers?'

'Yes indeed. Some – lunatics – broke in and sprayed acid over a number of club members.' Lark closed his eyes as if to shut out a hideous vision. She had an uncomfortable impression that he was fighting back tears. 'The one who died suffered from a chronic heart disease, and the shock – *killed* him.'

'That's – dreadful.'

'It is indeed. And hardly – a recommendation.'

'I don't quite understand you,' Hilary said.

92

Lark was standing almost too close, as if to prevent her from moving in any direction without pushing past him. He gave a strange impression that he was growing bigger, taller, monstrous. His eyes seemed to glow. *Hypnotic*, she thought, and narrowed her own eyes; it wouldn't help to look away, to make it obvious she was evading his gaze. He hadn't touched her nor shown any signs of touching her.

'You need – company and young friends of both sexes.'

'I – I daresay I do.'

'Normally – normally this club, the Lark Club, would be the ideal place for you.'

'Oh. I see.'

'However, in view – in view of this distressing occurrence you may not feel inclined to seek help from it.'

'Well,' Hilary said quietly, as if weighing up the pros and cons, 'I suppose such a happening is an isolated case, and it's hardly likely to occur *every* night.'

'No indeed,' he said. 'I—' he broke off, as if gathering his thoughts. 'Miss Reed, let me be very frank with you. I cannot and do not pretend to know exactly what you need. I would have to see you more often, keep you under observation – not medically, not physically, but – generally. I would need to find out how you react to other people, to temptations of all kinds, to pleasures of all kinds. The Lark Club is, as you may guess, a form of Therapy Club. In it membership means helping one another. New members mix with old ones, very soon they make friends, and one discovers – *I* discover – the people with whom they have much in common, a *rapport*, so to speak. We have private film shows, travelogues, games of infinite variety, lectures, experiments, fashion shows; we have an indoor swimming pool, and facilities for hobbies of all kinds. If you become one of us, then in a month's time I will have many reports on your characteristics and will be able to form an opinion about what you need to make you happy. And happiness is the objective of all human beings, Miss Reed. If only we could point an infallible way to human happiness!'

Hilary said practically: 'How expensive is it?'

'To join the Lark Club? Only five guineas for a year. To take part in the other and varied activites, much more, but these are a matter of your own choice. If you were with us for three months taking *all* advantages of our facilities, it would cost some two hundred and fifty pounds. You are not *poor*, Miss Reed, are you?'

'Not – not really poor.'

'Because we have a scheme by which we can help those who cannot afford the help they need . . .'

Lark began to explain in great detail, still standing close to Hilary Reed.

Roger, sitting in the front room at Bell Street, a whisky and soda by his side and all the daily newspapers spread about him, heard Janet talking to a neighbour in the garden, and wondered whether he was justified in still using his tender shoulder as an excuse not to mow the grass. Deciding regretfully that he was not, he was about to get up and start work when the telephone bell rang. There was an extension at his left hand.

'Roger West.'

'Moriarty here, sir!'

'Yes,' Roger said crisply.

'Detective Constable Reed's here, with a *very* interesting report.'

'Where's here?' asked Roger.

'At the Yard, sir.'

Roger hesitated, and then said:

'Tell her to come over and report to me at my home – and she shouldn't be in uniform.'

'Right, sir! Lark seems to have been very upset by the death of that man after the attack. *Can* we bring that in as murder?'

'I don't know,' Roger said. 'I'm consulting the Solicitor's Department.'

He thought Moriarty said something under his breath, but his response came smoothly, even silkily.

'Better be safe than sorry, sir!'

Roger went into the kitchen to tell Janet the girl would be coming.

'So now you can't *possibly* cut the grass,' Janet said, but she was laughing. 'It's all right, darling, Richard's got a day off tomorrow and he'll do it then.'

Half an hour later, Hilary Reed pulled up outside the house at the wheel of a green TR3. Janet, at the window, saw the girl get out. There was an unmistakable poise about Hilary Reed, an air of breeding, grace, confidence.

'Don't tell me she's a *cop*,' gasped Janet.

'Do let her in,' said Roger, 'but don't let your jealousy blast her.'

'Beast.'

'Miaow!'

There were pleasant exchanges at the door as the girl entered. She was beautifully made-up, and dressed in a simple frock of jade green, trimmed with brown silk. Murmuring 'garden' Janet slipped away, leaving her to Roger. He took over easily, wondering who the make-up was for, and suggesting a drink.

'No thank you, sir.'

'No need to refuse for formality's sake.'

'I make it a rule never to drink while driving,' Hilary Reed told him.

'Sensible girl. Well, now, what happened?'

She reported with a brevity and lucidity he liked, and gave him a typewritten transcription of everything that had taken place. Then she went on:

'He is a strange man, sir, but I certainly had the impression that he was absolutely sincere in everything he said.'

'All the same he could have been inviting you to join one of the nastiest types of club.'

'Yes, I know – yet I think he *wanted* to help. And I think he was genuinely upset by what had happened. There is one thing I think we will have to face, sir.'

'What thing in particular?' Roger asked.

'I'm not sure he can be easily fooled.'

'Do you think he may have spotted you already?'

'I doubt it yet, but I think if I'm going to join the club I should become a full-time member, and not contrive to do routine work at the Yard while fitting in the club at odd times. And I think I should stay away from the Yard altogether if I do join, sir, and report daily by telephone.'

Roger thought: She's doing a Moriarty on me.

Aloud, he said: 'This could be a very dangerous business indeed. Sulphuric acid isn't a form of make-up.'

Quite calmly, Hilary Reed said: 'I'm grateful for the chance of working on this particular case, sir.'

'Are you? Why?'

'I joined the Force because I thought I could help in preventing crime among girls – in fact all young people,' she said. 'I didn't anticipate spending so much of my time dealing with perverted old men.'

'Who in turn pervert youngsters,' Roger pointed out mildly.

Hilary Reed didn't answer.

Roger thought irritably: What's the matter with the Force? Have we all become reformers? He looked very straightly into the girl's clear blue eyes, and said:

'First and last, we hunt criminals, Constable. Don't ever forget that.'

'I certainly won't sir.'

'Lark may possibly be genuine and sincere, or he may run his own particular kind of vice-and-brothel. He may even be crazy – it wouldn't over surprise me if someone in this affair is trying to play God. Or he may be the heart of some criminal activity, with someone else after him to cut his throat. There's nothing much more vicious than thieves falling out. Is all that clear?'

'Very clear, sir.' Her gaze was unwavering.

'Good. I want to know in detail what goes on at the Lark Club and the Lark Clinic. We've a long list of members and we'll check them all, one by one. You join, full time. Your instructions are to get all the information you can, but don't for heaven's sake play the heroine. If there's danger, get out – fast.' He stood up abruptly. 'These are orders, Miss Reed.'

'I understand fully, sir,' she said. 'I'm not exactly anxious to spoil my complexion.' She stood up, and Roger walked with her to the door and watched her drive off; no one would suspect that she was a policewoman, that was part of her usefulness. He saw Richard loping along on the other side of the street; saw, at the same time, a cyclist start off from the kerb. Seized by sharp, unreasoning fear, he shouted: *'Fish!'* at the top of his voice and saw his son spin round to confront the cyclist, who had something in his hand. Roger thought with horror: *It will hit him in the face!* Then he saw Richard drop down, saw something pass over his head, and strike a tree. There was a *plop!* of sound, and a cloud of vapour. Richard straightened up in a flash. As the cyclist wobbled, momentarily out of control, Richard launched himself forward like a cata-

96

pult, grabbed at the rider, missed, kicked out at the rear wheel, missed, and leapt through the air in a despairing final effort.

Then Roger saw Hilary Reed, swinging round at the wheel of her car. One moment she was at the end of the road, the next she was doing a U-turn, and instead of completing it she stayed in the middle of the road as the cyclist raced towards her, his head down, intent only on escaping from Richard.

'Look out!' screamed Richard, in anticipation.

'*God!*' gasped Roger.

Janet came rushing from the house.

'What is it? *What is it?*'

Hilary Reed put her hand on the horn and held it there, a dozen people working in their gardens turned to gape.

The cyclist saw the green car too late.

He smashed into the back of it, went flying ten feet or more into the air, curving an arc as of one performing a beautiful acrobatic trick, before hurtling towards the ground. He fell head first. Someone screamed, a strange eerie sound piercing the silence.

Richard, still running, managed to check his flight, reaching the little car, staring beyond Hilary Reed. When Roger reached them they were clutching each other as if instinctively needing the warmth of another human being to enable them to bear the shocking sight that met their eyes.

CHAPTER FOURTEEN

NIGHT OF TERROR

NIGHT settled slowly, warmly, over London.

At Chelsea, Richard went to bed but not to sleep, haunted by what he had seen; across the landing Janet lay awake, haunted by what might have happened to her son. In St John's Wood, where she did in fact live with her mother, Hilary Reed slept fitfully, for that had been her worst experience since she had joined the Force. In the room beneath Moriarty's Helena Young slept soundly, without drugs; in the room above, Moriarty stared blankly at a typewritten sheet of paper, aching for spectacular results, sure that Superintendent West would not get them. In the hospital at Putney Wainwright slept on his stomach, under sedation; in her tiny room next to Daisy's Jill Hickersley slept, lightly drugged. At Shepherd's Bush Betty Smith and Jonathan Cobden had not entirely forgotten but were no longer troubled by memory of the attack on them.

John Smith *alias* Osgood slept in his cell.

The man who would not give his name slept at Brixton Prison, where he had been sent on remand.

In the morgue the dead youth lay unnamed, with no one to claim him, only the marks on his body for identification.

As midnight approached, the lovers crept from their seclusion and came out of the shadows into the dim light of streets and cars. The police, tense until that time, began to slacken in their anxiety, for by midnight most of those who sought each other in love and desire were indoors, or very near their homes. Some were sad, some content, some elated, some a little fearful for what they had done and what might befall them.

But not *all* the lovers went home, for the night was warm and seductive, and for those who were alone, or lived with parents who believed in letting their children lead their own lives, there was no hurry. Like the police they had vanquished the thought of danger, and were oblivious of everyone except their mates.

Slowly, youths carrying spray guns moved through the darkness towards their victims.

One after another they reached positions from which they could attack.

Suddenly, the dark places were vivid with flashes of light and the silent places were shrill with the sound of screams. The police, shocked back into vigilance, suddenly came to life. Engines roared, and telephones began to ring, urgent and insistent, in police stations and hospitals; soon the ambulance sirens moaned through the streets, clanging an urgent warning.

Roger's telephone bell rang, and Janet, only just asleep, awoke suddenly.

Roger plucked up the receiver by the bedside.

'West,' he said, abruptly.

'Approximately fifty cases of acid burning reported, sir,' announced the Inspector in charge of Information. 'I knew you would wish to be informed.'

'Know where to find Moriarty?' demanded Roger, one leg already out of bed.

'Yes, sir.'

'Send for him at once – I'll be along in twenty minutes.' As Roger rang off, the light from street lamps was enough to show him Janet's sleepless eyes. 'Bad night for young lovers,' he remarked. 'Sorry, sweet, but I must go.'

'Roger!' Janet called, as he went downstairs. 'Be careful.'

Be careful.

By half past two, the reports stopped coming in. Roger, jacket off and tie hanging loose, Moriarty immaculate as ever, and two detective sergeants finished sticking pins in the locations on the map where the attacks had taken place. There had been seventy-three in twenty-eight different locations – from Clapham Common to Hampstead Heath, from Ham Common to Regent's Park, from Dulwich Common to Camberwell Green, from Ealing Common to the banks of the river along its leaf-lined length. Moriarty, darting like a lizard, made rough graph upon graph, list upon list, while Roger studied the Divisions and the nature of the reports.

They came in some variety.

Minor injuries, neither party detained in hospital.

Serious body burns, both parties detained in hospital.

Minor head and hair burns, young woman suffering from severe shock.

Serious hand burns . . .

Minor burns on lower torso . . .

Roger listed them, fearful of word of another death but so far no injury seemed fatally serious. There were other reports.

Book of Lark Club matches found near scene of assault.

Plastic Amo spray gun half full of sulphuric acid found.

Plastic glove found, fabric section burned – being examined for fingerprints.

Set of footprints found.

Footprints – spray guns – Lark Club matches; minor burns, serious burns, girl in shock, man in shock. So the tally went on. Moriarty kept coming across with sketches of the radius of the spray.

'Very much the same in every case, sir. Same kind of gun – a brand called Amo.'

'Better get all the acid samples here by morning and make sure they are all the same strength of acid,' said Roger. 'If they're from the same drum, it must have been quite a drum.'

'I'll fix it, sir.'

'And don't ask the Laboratory to give this priority over everything,' Roger warned. 'Just ask 'em to be as quick as they can.'

'But it *is* priority!' protested Moriarty.

'Not to them it isn't,' Roger said. 'Did you notice the timing?'

'About one third at half past eleven, one third at twelve, one third at twelve-thirty,' Moriarty answered.

'Yes. And the places,' went on Roger, while Moriarty looked puzzled. 'There was time for the attackers to move from here—' Roger pointed to Hampstead Heath – 'to there.' He stabbed at Regent's Park. 'It looks like three platoons of twenty-five pairs or so, operating three different raids.'

'I hadn't noticed that,' confessed Moriarty. 'So if there were two or more in each attack, there were at least fifty men in each.'

'Between fifty and a hundred, say.' Roger glanced at some statements. 'Any cycle tracks?'

'Not near the scenes of the attacks.'

'Better send word to have the approaches and all surrounding grass areas checked,' Roger advised. 'They may have used bicycles.' He shut his eyes to a momentary vision. 'No photograph spools or flash light bulbs?'

'No.'

Roger said: 'They use the built-in flash, then, and they're very expensive. There are a lot of them – it's not a question of one man and a few supporters playing God, it's on too big a scale. They must work from a centre, such as the Lark Club, but I doubt if it's from the Lark Club itself. We need to find where they're buying the spray guns and the acid – my God, we want to get busy!'

'Couldn't agree more, sir,' Moriarty said. 'I'll stay with it all night.'

Now he's waking up, Moriarty thought; but he can't blame me if it's too late.

They both stayed with it all night, with a staff which planned every move for the next day: a call at all suppliers of acid and of Amo spray guns, and manufacturers and wholesalers, calls on all social clubs, all known gangs of all ages, all suppliers of the built-in photographic flashes. Roger, red-eyed but still alert, approved the final General Call to the Divisions, just after seven o'clock.

'We'll break for breakfast,' he said to Moriarty, when that was done.

'I'm all right, sir.'

Roger thought: I mustn't keep on nagging him, and forbore to advise him to get some rest and not to overdo it. By the time he himself had shaved, showered, and had breakfast, the morning papers were in. The *Daily Globe*'s headline screamed: NIGHT OF TERROR.

Five newspapers took the same line, the *Echo* doing a magnificent job with a map taking up a whole page, and indicating the scene of every crime. The more Roger studied this, the more he realized the magnitude of the attacks. It was half past nine when the telephone bell rang in Roger's office; it was Pengelly.

'You could have called me,' he said reproachfully.

'Took it for granted you'd be told,' Roger said, and added with a surge of honesty: 'As a matter of fact, Pen, I didn't give you a thought.'

'That's more like the truth,' said Pengelly. 'There's one thing now, Handsome.'

'What's that?'

'For the next few nights there will hardly be a loving couple in London's parks and open spaces after dark.'

'You may be right,' conceded Roger.

'I'm right, all right,' insisted Pengelly. 'If these people are out for a clean-up operation they've found the right way to do it.'

'Haven't got any inside news, have you?' demanded Roger. 'No.'

'I've an idea,' Roger said musingly.

'What is it?'

'Do you think your paper might offer a substantial reward to anyone giving information?' Roger asked. 'We can't offer a big enough one, and most of the newspapers would be nervous – we're going to get a surprising number of self-righteous folk saying that the end justifies the means. Some of the newspapers will be afraid of upsetting the more narrow-minded readers and the bigots, but your people might take a chance.'

'If,' said Pengelly cryptically.

'If what?' demanded Roger.

'If we could be sure of getting the Yard's story first,' said Pengelly. 'For instance, I saw one of your questionnaires at North West Division this morning. Very much to the point if I may say so. You didn't send any out to the Press, did you?'

'No.'

'Why not let us print it this evening and tomorrow? I know you can't give us exclusive rights but you could give us a head start. And if we can induce one of the acid sprayers to talk, you might be able to break the case right open.'

'I'll see about it,' Roger said. 'I'll call you back.'

'Why not let the *Evening Globe* buy you a lunch?' suggested Pengelly. 'Danelli's, say, at one o'clock.'

'I'll be there if I don't send a message,' Roger promised.

Coppell turned up his nose.

'You know we have to be very careful not to give one newspaper any advantage over the others, West.'

'We have done, before,' Roger reminded him.

'But over this—' Coppell sounded coldly disapproving.

'I know it's a delicate situation,' Roger said stubbornly, 'but if we can get the full support of the *Evening Globe* it could help us in the general investigation into all the crimes. Once it commits itself, the *Globe* can help a great deal. If they do a few editorials saying they're all along the line with us on a general cleaning up campaign—' he broke off, aware that he shouldn't have said that; a 'cleaning up' campaign wasn't likely to appeal to Coppell or the other top brass of the Yard.

Coppell gave one of his rare, considered smiles.

'Need a different title,' he observed. 'Think about it, and see what Pengelly suggests. Don't make the Yard out to be a kind of Protector of the Public Morals – we're just protectors of the public property. But—' he hesitated, then stood up and moved to his window, from which he could see the Houses of Parliament. 'West,' he went on in an aloof voice, 'I can't possibly approve this – you know that. However, if Pengelly and the *Globe* want to go along, I can't stop it. You must use your own judgement.' Slowly, almost painfully, he added: 'If you see what I mean.'

Roger saw exactly what he meant.

'What it amounts to is this,' he said to Pengelly as they sat in a secluded corner of Danelli's, a pleasant restaurant on the river not far from the Yard. 'Coppell won't give me any backing. If I let you have information ahead of the others and there's a row, I'll get the caning.'

'Mean old so-and-so,' said Pengelly. He had a schoolmaster's look, a schoolmaster's steel-rimmed glasses, a touch of severe benevolence about his face, which was not unlike Josiah Lark's. 'We'll do all we can to make sure no one knows where we got our information from. You know that.'

'Yes,' agreed Roger. 'My problem is to decide whether the help you can give justifies my sticking my neck out.'

'We'll pledge full support,' Pengelly assured him. 'I saw the editor and the editor saw the Old Man and the Old Man's a great one for the freedom of the individual and people doing what they do because they think it's right, not because they're made to say it is or are under compulsion to do it. Teach 'em, don't make 'em. That's his motto, and this fits in with the idea. As if you didn't know,' added Pengelly drily.

Roger's eyes glistened.

'There's the heading – the theme,' he said. 'Teach Them – Don't Make Them – Don't Scare Them. *Teach* the young the follies of fornication, don't frighten them away from it or they'll get mad, and they'll lust after it. How does that sound?' His voice and his expression were eager.

Pengelly sat back and took off his glasses; his eyes were like pebbles.

'You're wasted at the Yard,' he declared. 'Yes, you should have been on the Street. That will be our leading article to-night. A restrained attack on the men behind these attacks without approving the practice of proliferating in the parks.' He rubbed his eyes. 'Anything else, Handsome?'

'It almost looks as if someone could be playing God,' Roger said with a deprecating smile.

Pengelly sniffed. 'I know what you mean. I don't think we'll touch that angle yet, though – except to allow it to speak for itself.'

'Pen,' Roger said, 'it could be a very important angle for us.'

'Meaning you want us to use it?'

'As soon as you can.'

'All right, I'll see what I can do,' promised Pengelly.

'And how about a reward for any information leading to the capture of the leader of the acid sprayers?' asked Roger.

'I've fixed that. One thousand pounds,' said Pengelly, with an air of great nonchalance.

'Pen,' Roger said, 'Whenever I can do anything for you, believe me I will.'

Pengelly looked up at a waiter who had the face of an Adonis, said: 'What?' and then added hastily: 'Yes, take it away.' The waiter took the plates and the black pepper they had had for smoked salmon, and Pengelly put his glasses on.

'I'll remind you of that,' he said. 'So there were an estimated twenty-five to thirty different small parties worked last night,' he remarked.

'Yes.'

'What do you mean – one man playing God and between fifty and a hundred disciples helping him in his s-praying?' When Roger didn't answer, Pengelly went on: 'You can't seriously believe that as many young louts as that could be organized into an acid-spraying army because they think it's the right thing to do. They're *paid* to do this, or else they do it for sheer devilment. A mixture of the two, I shouldn't wonder. I'll run your tirade against a man playing God if you like, but you and I don't think that's the man we're looking for.'

'I don't know who I'm looking for,' confessed Roger.

The young Adonis arrived with *bœuf stroganoff* for Roger, sole grilled on the bone for Pengelly, and they set to. As they finished Danelli himself, short, plump, smiling his Italian smile, came up with a copy of the *Evening News*.

'Your picture on it, Mr West, I think you like to see,' he said. 'You forgive me, Mr Pengelly, if it is the wrong paper.'

'Surprised you have this rag in the place,' joked Pengelly. 'I – what's up, Roger?'

Danelli looked aghast at Roger's expression.

His photograph was there. So was Jill Hickersley's appealing, heart-shaped face. So was an Identi-kit picture, beneath which the caption read: An Identi-kit picture by Yard experts of Clive Davidson based on information given by Jill Hickersley (photo inset).

CHAPTER FIFTEEN

RAGE

WHITE-FACED, more angry than he had been for years, Roger strode into the room where Moriarty was working with two Detective Sergeants. The sergeants took one look at Roger, and dived out. Roger banged the door to, slammed the newspaper on Moriarty's desk, and demanded in a taut voice:

'Did you release that picture of Davidson?'

'Yes, I—'

'And that story?'

'Yes, I thought—'

'Moriarty,' Roger said, savagely, 'you *can't* think. Not yet. You can't *begin* to think. And you can't obey orders. I told you not to release that picture without my express permission – *didn't* I?'

'Yes, but—'

'There aren't any buts. You deliberately disobeyed, and I know *why* you disobeyed.' Roger leaned forward on the desk, arms spread, hands clutching the edge, looking down at the younger man, whose face had lost all colour, and whose eyes were like dark blue glass. 'You don't think I'm handling this case properly. You don't think I'm quick enough off the mark.' He paused, to give Moriarty a chance to fling back: 'No I don't,' but the other sat absolutely still, his lips parted just enough to show his teeth; it was almost as if he were snarling. 'You think you can do the job better than I can. Well, get this into your head. You've betrayed a young girl witness who's had a rotten deal already. You've made *me* out a liar. You've destroyed any faith she ever had in the police. She might become a vital witness – why, you bloody young fool, don't you realize she's the *only* person who can identify Clive Davidson? The YMCA staff can't swear who was with her that night and who ran away. Only *she* can. Think she's likely to, now?' he rasped. 'Come on, tell me – do you think she's likely to?'

Moriarty ground out: 'If we make her.'

'We aren't going to *make* her. We can't *make* people do anything. We need witnesses who want to help us. If we have the biggest criminal in London in front of us we can't *make*

105

him tell the truth – we never will be able to. But whether this girl's evidence is important or not, we've broken faith – the Yard with her, and you with me. No officer who works for me breaks faith. I tell him what to do and he does it. If there's ever any need to use his own judgement I tell him his terms of reference in advance. That's how we work at the Yard – in the Force. Any other way would lead to anarchy. You've been in the Force twelve years, haven't you learned that elementary rule?'

He stopped, partly for breath, partly because his anger was beginning to cool off now that he had vented so much of it. Nothing stirred in the office. The piles of papers on Moriarty's desk and on a table alongside one wall, the annotated maps and charts showed how much work this man had done, but thought of that did nothing to ease Roger's tension.

Moriarty shifted his chair back a few inches, and spoke between his teeth.

'Want my resignation – sir?'

'When I want you off the job I'll fire you.'

Moriarty drew in a hissing breath.

Roger said: 'Why did you do it? Come on, tell me.'

Moriarty moistened his lips but did not speak.

'Why?' rasped Roger.

'I – I used my own judgement.'

'Any special reason behind it?'

'No.' Moriarty drew in another, deeper breath, and said harshly: 'I thought you were wrong not to use the picture.'

'Just that?'

'Yes – sir.'

'So when I give you instructions you turn them over in your mind and decide whether you approve, and if you don't, you disobey them.' There was a pause. 'Is that right?'

Moriarty remarked: *'I've* got a mind, too.'

'You're a police officer. You take orders. You take my orders. From now on your duty is to take them without argument – unless I *ask* you to argue. If I want your opinion I'll ask for it. If you've an opinion you think is worth expressing, you tell me about it – you don't *act* on it without authority. Is that clear?'

Moriarty said hoarsely: 'Yes – sir.'

'At half past three I'll be in my office. At half past three I want you there. Then you can tell me whether you understand the position and accept it. If you don't you can go back to Division. If you accept it and break the rules again I'll recommend you for retirement forthwith as an officer incapable of submitting to discipline. Is that clear?'

'Ye-yes.'

For the first time, Roger drew back.

'Are all up-to-the-minute reports on my desk?'

'Yes, sir.'

'Nothing new is in except what's there?'

'No.'

Roger nodded, turned, and strode out. He walked with long, aggressive strides to his office, nodding brusquely to those who acknowledged him on the way. He went in, stared out the clear window at the slow-moving pageant of the river, lips set, chin thrust forward, still angry.

Moriarty's cheeks were grey, his lips pale, his eyes like molten glass, his hands clenched, his body stiff as steel. He kept muttering: 'The swine, the bloody swine, the bloody swine, the bloody bloody swine.'

At last Roger's tension eased out, and a restless calm took its place. He moved to his desk, dropped into the chair and began to go through the accumulation of reports. On top were three from Moriarty, neatly typewritten, lucid, on the ball; everything Roger had ordered last night had been done, the requests were out, a few replies were coming in. For instance:

Two Lark Club match books had been found near the scene of the attacks.

Eleven lots of bicycle tyre prints had been found but none positively associated with the assailants.

Four policemen and seven people who had been in the parks and commons around the time of the crimes had *seen* cyclists nearby at the time.

So far there were no reports of a substantial number of Amo spray guns having been sold; dozens of carboys and drums of concentrated sulphuric acid had been bought and sold, and over seven hundred factories in the Central and Greater London areas held stocks of the acid. All were being checked, through the Divisions.

Moriarty hadn't missed a thing.

Roger sat back and lit a cigarette. He felt curiously deflated, and was reminded of his moods when he had torn strips off the boys, often with Janet watching in silent disapproval. Sometimes he had gone too far; that was the danger when one usually held oneself on a leash. Janet had been so much more with the boys than he, he'd usually left their handling to her. Often he'd been over-tired when he had let himself go. He was over-tired now; so was Moriarty, who couldn't have had much sleep for days.

'Don't be a fool,' he adjured himself. 'Moriarty's got this know-all streak and it's got to be knocked out of him.'

It was a little after three o'clock. He wished there were some time to go out to Chelsea and see Jill Hickersley, but he was probably worrying too much about that. He made two or three divisional calls before the Laboratory rang down.

'All the acid's from the same batch, Handsome.'

'Meaning – the same drum or container?'

'No – meaning the same batch. There are a dozen manufacturers, and every batch each one makes would be exactly the same, whether it was a hundred or a thousand gallons.'

'Any idea of the manufacturer?'

'I think it's Webb, Son, and King, of Wandsworth.'

'Thanks,' Roger said. He rang off and was about to make another call when the bell rang. 'Yes?'

'Front hall here, sir,' a man said. 'There's a Miss Hickersley asking to see you.'

'Jill Hickersley?' Roger had a vivid glimpse of that heart-shaped face.

'Just a moment, sir . . . Yes, that's right.'

'I'll send for her,' Roger said. He rang for a messenger to fetch the girl, wondering whether she had come simply in reproach. Somehow, he didn't think so. When the messenger ushered her in, Roger was at his desk, noticing how small and neat and wholesome she was and remembering how roughly she had been stripped. He was probably fooling himself; the most virginal and serene-looking young girls could be harridans and termagants; he must not allow himself to be over sympathetic.

He shook hands gravely.

'I'm afraid I owe you a very sincere apology.'

'Why *did* you release that picture?' she asked, eyeing him steadily.

'Do you want the simple truth?' Roger asked.

'Of course.'

'It was a mistake by someone here.'

She frowned. 'You mean you didn't intend to release it?'

'Certainly not. There was a misunderstanding among my men.'

'Oh,' she said, and seemed to droop. 'Then I—' she half-laughed in a rueful way. 'I felt so sure you wouldn't have released it unless there was an emergency and I wondered what the emergency was. You see—' she hesitated.

'Yes?'

Her eyes were violet.

'I – can I speak in confidence, Superintendent?'

'In absolute confidence,' he assured her.

'Well, I've been thinking a great deal about – about what happened, and why it did, and why Clive should disappear. If it's connected with this acid-throwing, and I guessed it was because you're in charge of that investigation, then it's obviously very important.'

Roger said cautiously : 'It certainly could be.'

'You see, I—' She hesitated, her colour heightened. 'I feel disloyal, in a way, but I can't believe that Clive is in any way involved, so he *could* be in danger, couldn't he?'

'When a man runs away in any such emergency he's usually either ashamed or scared, and they amount to the same thing.'

'Superintendent, he is an industrial chemist, and he works for a firm called Webb, Son, and King, of Wandsworth. There – there was a case of acid burning a few weeks ago, you may remember, and he said then that his company makes sulphuric acid. He told me quite a lot about it – the fact that the man who uses it must know what he is doing, that most metal sprays or guns would be damaged by the acid, and that a special kind of plastic would have to be used – called polyethyl, or something like that. He – he really seemed interested and concerned and I thought – well, I thought you should know this, and – I thought you would tell me *why* you'd released his picture if I told you.' She gave a little laugh. 'It was silly, wasn't it?'

'It was very wise indeed. I'll check with this firm right away.' Roger rang Moriarty, and spoke as if nothing had

109

happened. 'Telephone Webb, Son, and King, of Wandsworth, they're chemical manufacturers, and find out if Clive Davidson is on their staff, and whether he's in today.'

'Er—' said Moriarty.

Roger thought: He's not still at it!

'Yes?' he asked sharply.

'I had a call from the firm five minutes ago, sir. They recognized him from the picture in the *Evening News*.'

Now Moriarty would have every excuse if he wanted to gloat.

'What else?' asked Roger.

'He hasn't been in for two days, sir. Didn't say he'd be away and no one's telephoned. He works in the laboratory.'

'I see. Send over some samples of the sulphuric acid we have in the lab. and ask them to check if it came from them, and if so can they tell us what batch.'

'Right, sir.'

'And make it three-forty-five when you come here.'

'Yes, sir.'

Roger rang off. The girl sat very upright, very prim, facing him. Her eyes looked enormous. She did not stir as he told her what Moriarty had already discovered, and he wondered what was going on behind those nice eyes, whether she had told him everything she could. *Make* her, Moriarty had said, and would most certainly have tried to.

'So Clive is involved,' she said at last.

'He could be, obviously.'

'Mr – Mr West.'

'Yes?'

'Do you think he has been injured?'

Slowly, Roger asked: 'Do you mean, do I think he might be dead?'

'It – it *has* occurred to me. I – that's what I'm so desperately anxious to know. You see—' She bit her lip, and then went on: 'Until he disappeared and I began to get worried, I didn't really know what I felt, but I do now. I hope it doesn't sound silly. I'm in love with him. You *don't* think he's been killed, do you?'

Gently, Roger replied: 'All I know is that he appears to be missing. We'll have his address soon, and if we get any information, we will let you know.'

110

She stood up, accepting the dismissal.

'Thank you very much,' she said warmly.

Roger walked along the passage with her and to the top of the high stone steps, watched her graceful going, then turned, to find the duty sergeant doing likewise. Each man smiled. Pretty little thing, they said with their eyes, and with a whiff of nostalgia for their own youth. Roger went back to his office, and hadn't been there more than half a minute before the telephone bell rang.

'West.'

'Moriarty, sir. They've found something to suggest that a man may have been killed in one of the acid tanks at Webb, Son, and King's. Should we take those acid samples over?'

CHAPTER SIXTEEN

TRACES

THE OLD building, of blackened brick with a grey slate roof, was near the river at Wandsworth. There was an unpleasant, rather sulphurous odour which came downwind and made Roger feel sick. Tall chimneys rose at one side and there was some scaffolding round one of these. The approach was over a cobbled, now tarred-over road, the surface of which was wearing so thin that cobbles showed through. The double doors of the entrance were at one end; beyond was a long passage with offices branching off. Typewriters clattered, someone was talking on a telephone, another telephone bell rang.

Roger stopped at a window marked Inquiries. A youth, probably a good deal sharper than he looked, said quietly:

'Can I help you?'

Roger showed his card.

'I want to see Mr Menzies, the Works Manager. He's expecting me.'

The youth read the card painstakingly.

'He's in the works, I gotta take you.'

He led the way, Roger on his heels, Moriarty just behind. They went through a small green-painted door into a large, hangar-like factory, where the smell they had noticed outside was much stronger.

All round the walls were enormous tanks, and on the wall at a level with the tops of these tanks was a wide platform, rather like a mezzanine floor, approached by open staircases at each corner. Even from floor level Roger could see the manholes at each tank and pipes leading down to it, feeding from above. Beneath the tanks was a deep pit which ran round the walls on three sides with ramps up to floor level. The pit contained metal drums and glass carboys which could be filled from faucets at the bottom of the tanks. Both the platform and the pit were protected by sturdy wire fences.

Roger, Moriarty, and the youth hovered about a little group of men, the central figure of which was big, broad, florid, with thick lips and a bulbous, veinous nose. Two of the men were wearing dark-blue boiler suits and masks. Both the masks, and the stench, surprised Roger, for concentrated sulphuric acid was odourless and did not evaporate.

The big man was saying in a deep, unexpectedly mellow voice:

'Well get up there again and make sure it's empty – bloody stuff will start leaking all over the neighbourhood if we're not careful.' He turned to Roger, saying: 'Had a leak in the ovens, that's what's making the stink. Want masks?'

'I can manage,' Roger said, and Moriarty nodded.

'*Handsome* of you,' the man said, and grinned. 'I'm Menzies, the works manager.' He had a big hand and a strong grip. 'I'd recognize you anywhere, Superintendent. Nasty business, this.'

'What is?' asked Roger.

'No one told you?'

'Not in detail.'

'We emptied the tank because of the leak; it would be full of sulphur and a hell of a lot of impurities. The acid was no good. We found more residue than we expected,' went on Menzies. 'See that?' He pointed to the sludge in a big tray on the floor of the pit beneath the tank. 'Found a gold pencil, the strap of a watch, plastic shoelaces, and a few other odds and ends, including a diamond,'

Roger asked quickly: 'Have you facilities for finding out what that sludge is made of?'

'Tests are being made,' answered Menzies. One of the men in uniform spoke, and Menzies barked: 'What's that, Jones? Speak up man!'

'Gold fillings, sir – some gold fillings.'

'And a bridge,' another said.

'Metal dental bridge – yes.' Menzies narrowed his bloodshot eyes.

'When was the tank last emptied?' inquired Roger.

'Week ago – eh, Jones?'

'Week ago to the minute, sir. Routine, it is.'

'Anyone else on your staff missing?' asked Roger.

'Not that I know of – and *I'd* know.'

'How could a man fall in?'

'Couldn't, unless he'd opened up the manhole on the platform and jumped. Or someone else had opened up the manhole, and pushed.' The man was quite matter-of-fact.

'You're suggesting suicide or murder?'

'Couldn't have been an accident – could it, Jones?'

'Impossible, sir.' Jones was an echo.

'Like to see the works – know what I'm talking about then,' said Menzies, and taking their consent for granted he started towards a big open lift. A man opened the criss-cross gates. 'The ovens where we burn the sulphur are up top ... these sacks are of sulphur ... burn the stuff to sulphor trioxide and the gas is absorbed in water or a weak acid and the concentrated sulphuric runs down pipes into these big tanks.'

On the top floor he showed the big stocks of sulphur in paper sacks, fed mechanically into the ovens. Beneath the ovens were the pipes leading into the tanks on the platform floor. They went down an open staircase on to this platform. The top of the tank was in fact on a level with it, and at each tank, fed from above by the huge pipes, was a larger manhole than Roger had seen from the floor.

Menzies led the way to one which stood open.

'This is it,' he announced. 'These manholes are kept closed except when we're clearing the tanks, or testing them for strength or impurities.' He pointed to two steel bars across the manhole. 'We have to keep these bars in position under the Factory Safety Act, unless a man needs to go down into one when it's empty. You've just been into this, haven't you, Jones?'

'Yes, sir.'

'When the tank's full of acid it's sealed until we draw it off into the containers in the pit,' went on Menzies. 'You can see them over there.' He turned and pointed to tanks on the other side of the factory. 'See the big faucet at the bottom? . . . And those steel drums? . . . and the carboys. All very simple, really. We burn the sulphur on the roof, and mix it with water or a weak acid, run it down into the tanks and store it there until it's ready to be shipped. The drums are rolled up the ramps, the carboys go on trolleys. Got that?'

'Pretty well,' said Roger.

Moriarty nodded, as if he understood perfectly.

'We'll go down, then.' They went back to the ground floor, and as they reached it Menzies demanded: 'What will you people want to do? Send in a Murder Team, hey? Question everybody – well, if it has to be it has to be, but make it as short as you can and interfere with work as little as possible. Got the weekend coming up but we're doing a seven-day week, even at double pay for some of the overtime.' In the pause which followed, his 'Eh, Jones?' seemed to hang in the air. Then: 'Jones, give the police all the assistance they want.'

'Certainly will, sir.'

Out of the corner of his eye Menzies saw another youth in a khaki smock approach, and swivelled round to meet him.

'What is it, son?'

'The pen and the watch strap,' the youth said.

'Well?'

'Mr Davidson's sir – three of the assistants all say so. And they think the diamond's from a ring Mr Davidson wore.'

'Keep it to yourselves, all of you. Keep mum. D'you hear?'

'Yes, sir.'

'That's an official police order,' Roger said to the youth, and added to Menzies: 'I'd like to take away everything that was found, as soon as possible.'

'I need a receipt, that's all,' said Menzies.

Roger hesitated, feeling that Menzies was intent on scoring a kind of victory at every stage. It might be that he was just a show-off, anxious to impress his men, but it might also be a betrayal of deepest nervousness. Moriarty was obviously champing with impatience, and this was a chance to give him his head.

'Call the Yard and ask for a team,' he said, 'and stay here with it until everything's done. Can you spare me a few minutes in your office, Mr Menzies?'

114

'If that's what you want, okay.'

Menzies had a box-like, tubular steel type office and a streamlined secretary who obviously knew him very well. She had an even tinier office adjoining and Roger noticed that the inter-office communicating box was not switched off; but there was nothing he wanted to prevent the girl from hearing.

'Well?' Menzies almost barked.

'Did Davidson ever appear to be in trouble, sir?'

'Only with wenches,' answered Menzies.

'Will you elaborate that, please.'

'He fancied himself as a lady's man – no pretty girl was safe from him. Good worker, though, certainly knew his onions – or rather his acids.' Menzies let out a great gust of laughter.

'Were any of the other men jealous of him, do you know?'

'No idea, Super.'

'Did he have any enemies that you know of?'

'No, no one special, anyway. Had a few irate fathers and a couple of angry husbands after him at various times, but he could always talk himself out of trouble. Quite a boy, our Clive.' Menzies spoke as if with envy.

'So it seems. Have you a photograph of him?'

'Oh, sure – in his file. We always have one with the applications for employment. Want it?'

'Yes, please. And what was his latest address?' Roger asked.

'My secretary will know – he was always changing, wanted to make sure he couldn't be found, half the time.'

'You're maligning his character pretty badly, sir.'

'Just telling you the truth, that's all,' said Menzies bluffly. 'You'd find it out sooner or later.'

'Did any of these irate husbands and fathers you mention ever come here?'

'Oh, several of them,' declared Menzies. 'The last time it happened I told him if we had any more trouble he could look for another job. I'm quite prepared to wink an eye at a man's peccadillos, provided they don't tangle up in his business, but he was often out late at night and next morning he would sometimes have to take a few hours off, in case someone came looking for him.'

'When did you deliver this ultimatum?' Roger wanted to know.

'Three days ago,' Menzies answered promptly. 'When he

115

didn't turn up next day I thought he'd taken the huff. No
telling what labour will do these days – pay 'em the earth, and
they turn their noses up at you.'

'Did you personally see these people who came here after
him, sir?'

'Some of them. My secretary saw them all. Why?'

'She may be able to identify the men we're anxious to interview, Mr Menzies.' Roger opened his brief-case and recalled
that it was Moriarty who had put in the batch of photographs.
'Can she come in for a few minutes?'

'Why not?' Menzies raised his voice. 'Patsy, come here,
love!' As Roger spread the photographs out on the black-
topped desk, the girl came in, with a certain slinky grace. She
stood rather close to him and he was subtly aware – as he was
sure she meant him to be – of her perfume, and of her long,
smooth, bare arms.

Her heavily darkened eyes widened.

'*He* was one of the first,' she said, and pointed at a photograph of Albert Young, Helena Young's father, who had
driven his daughter from home and his wife to the point of
suicide.

After a pause, and as she looked at him slyly, Roger asked:
'Are you absolutely sure?'

'Positive!' She was excited, seeing herself the centre of a
great drama.

'If necessary, would you swear to it in court?'

'Certainly I would.'

'Thank you very much,' Roger said. 'Keep it to yourself for
the time being, please.'

'Oh,' promised Patsy, half serious, half provocative, 'if you
say so, I won't say a *word*.'

She went out, a little wobbly on very high heels, thoroughly
pleased with herself. Menzies, who had remained silent for a
longer period than Roger had yet known, eyed her up and
down as she went out, and then said, in a deliberately carrying
voice:

'That girl doesn't miss a thing. The man Young was here all
right. Didn't see him myself, but you can rely on it. Next?'

'Who uses your concentrated sulphuric acid?'

'You mean, who'd carry some of our stocks? We've a couple
of hundred customers – ordinary stockists, factories who buy it

116

'or pickling – cleaning to you, sir.' He laughed. 'Small wool-
lyers, too. The biggest customers are fertilizer manufacturers,
t's used in ammonium sulphate – comes in powder or crys-
als.'

Roger nodded as he made mental notes, then asked:

'Can we go into your laboratory?'

'Be a good idea to shake 'em up. Let's go.'

The laboratory, like the office, was modern and well
equipped, the actual benches and equipment contrasting
strangely with the begrimed brick and the big iron girders
which spanned the roof. Half a dozen men, all very young, were
at work, including the young man who had come up to them at
the vats. One was elderly, however, and wore glasses with
thick lenses. In front of him were a number of test tubes,
slides, bell-jars, beakers, and the usual impedimenta of the
chemical laboratory.

'No doubt about it,' he said. 'They're human remains.' He
touched a yellow object with the end of a glass rod. 'That's a
gold tooth filling. No doubt about it at all.'

Moriarty was too busy here to be taken away from the factory.
Roger called the Putney Division from his car, ordered a close
watch on Albert Young, then telephoned the Yard for an investigation into Young's past, and into his daughter's *affaires*.
Satisfied, he left Moriarty in charge of the Murder Squad
which arrived from the Yard and from the Division, and went
back to the Yard. It was no use getting too impatient and
doing a Moriarty, but he wanted results now, feeling as if he
were on the verge of them.

The Yard laboratory confirmed that the remains in the vat
were human, and once the Press learned of this there would be
the tremendous sensation of an Acid Bath Murder campaign,
coming on top of the rest.

'It's too late for the *Evening Globe*,' Roger told Coppell.

'Use your own judgement,' Coppell said impatiently. 'I've
got to be off.'

So Roger called Pengelly.

'I've a big piece of news which might not keep,' he said. 'A
lot of people know of it, and someone will certainly let it out.'

'Let me know what it is and I'll sit on it,' Pengelly assured
him. He listened, then whistled. '*This* is really something,

Handsome. You won't divulge it to the mornings, will you?'

'Not unless my hand is forced,' Roger said. 'Do something else for me, will you?'

'Something *else*?'

'Get as detailed a story as you can on the love lives of Clive Davidson,' Roger said, 'and of Helena Young.'

'That child?' When Roger didn't answer, Pengelly said almost excitedly: 'A nod's as good as a wink. Okay, Handsome!'

As Roger rang off, he noticed a pencilled note on his desk: 'Detective Constable Hilary Reed called. She is at MAS 1432.' Immediately he put through a call, getting a vivid mental picture of the acid throwing in Bell Street, the way the cyclist had crashed into Hilary Reed's car, the awful sight which they had seen together.

She answered at once.

'Thank you for calling, Mr West. I've joined the Lark Club, and spent some hours there today. The first impression is wholly favourable.'

Roger said: 'Well, we only want the truth about it, good or bad. Try to find out if any of the following people have ever been members – they're not in the present membership list. Ready to take the names?'

'Yes, sir.'

'Helena Young,' Roger began, 'Albert Young, Clive Davidson—'

'Excuse me, sir,' Hilary interrupted, 'is this the list of people whose photographs we've just had printed?'

'Yes.'

'Chief Inspector Moriarty gave me a copy of the list and some passport size photographs,' the girl said. 'I'm studying them now.'

'Good!' Roger infused heartiness into his voice. 'Don't take them with you to the club.'

'I certainly won't, sir.'

'Have you noticed anything unusual yet?' Roger asked.

'There's a remarkable likeness between Albert Young and the club secretary, a man named Delafield,' Hilary Reed answered. 'I told Mr Moriarty, and he says we are checking for any relationship.'

'We are. And don't forget to be very careful,' Roger said. 'I'm serious about that.'

118

'I know, sir, and appreciate it,' the girl said. Her tone changed and she asked: 'How is your son, Richard? He's such a nice boy and it must have been a dreadful shock last night.'

'He'll get over it,' Roger said drily. 'He hopes your car wasn't damaged much.'

'Wasn't dam—' she echoed, and laughed. 'Then he's over it!'

She had an old head on her shoulders, Roger reflected; he had a feeling that she would be far less impetuous than Moriarty, but no less sure of herself.

He worked solidly for the next two hours; then one of the messengers brought in a copy of the *Evening Globe*. The Identi-kit picture of Clive Davidson was in this edition and a big front page story of the previous night's events, with a pointing finger at the end of it saying: See Editorial Page 8. He turned to the editorial, which was headed: TEACH THEM – DON'T SCARE THEM. It ran on:

One of the strangest campaigns in the history of this fine and ancient city is being waged – a campaign, we believe, by some self-righteous, God-fearing men and women against the loose morality of so many of today's youth.

But youth needs teaching and training, not frightening. Youth needs glowing examples of moral behaviour, not awful warnings.

The *Evening Globe* prints on another page a questionnaire circulated to all London police by Scotland Yard. It is an effort to analyse the categories of crimes committed by youth, and the homes from which the criminals come. The purpose is wholly commendable and the *Evening Globe* is wholeheartedly behind the police, BUT—

Youth must be taught what is RIGHT. And that is society's task, not the task of the police.

To help SOCIETY, this newspaper offers the sum of
£1,000 Reward
to any individual who gives the police any information which leads to the apprehension of the LEADERS of those ill-guided men who, by taking the law into their own hands, defeat the course of justice and so DEFEAT THE CAUSE OF YOUTH.

CHAPTER SEVENTEEN

NIGHT OF SILENCE

ROGER read the leader through twice, smiling grimly. Pengell
had done everything he had promised and very cleverly; even
Coppell at his most nervous could not complain. It was after
seven, and Roger pushed his chair back, thinking there should
soon be word from Moriarty. As he stifled a yawn, there was
tap at the door.

Moriarty came in, perhaps a little diffidently.

'Sorry I'm so late, sir.'

'How did things go at Webbs'?' asked Roger.

'Not much more to report,' Moriarty answered. 'Picked up
couple of dozen prints of size 9 and $9\frac{1}{2}$ shoes, any one of which
might be identical with the prints found on the common.' That
was thorough, Roger thought, if not particularly hopeful. 'I'
send them down for comparison,' Moriarty went on, standing
at ease. 'I checked with all the staff on duty, there's no doub
of Clive Davidson's reputation as a womanizer or of Alber
Young's outraged-father visit.'

'So Helena Young isn't the innocent she seemed.'

'Apparently not,' said Moriarty. 'I think I should talk t
her.'

'So do I.'

'Will you see Albert Young?' asked Moriarty.

'As soon as I know more about him – and we've got men o
the job.'

'Expect more trouble on the commons tonight, sir?'

'I don't know what to expect,' Roger said, 'but before you
go I want a special alert to all Divisions for a special watch
from an hour before darkness tonight. I want to know how
many couples go looking for seclusion, and what effect this i
going to have on them.'

'Most celibate night in the history of London, I'd say!'

'You could be right.' Roger shifted his chair back, an
paused; the younger man braced himself physically, shoulder
square, head high, chin out. Was it in defiance? Or was h
simply facing up to the situation? They looked at each othe

levelly for an appreciable time before Roger went on: 'Did I make myself clear this afternoon?'

'*Very* clear, sir.'

'Do you want to go on with this job?'

'Nothing I want more, sir.'

'Does the fact that we got results from the Identi-kit picture seem to you to justify its release?'

Moriarty hesitated. This was the crucial question and his response to it would really set the pattern for the future. Roger, imagining he could see the fire burning in those Irish eyes, sensing Moriarty's compulsive urge to act at all costs, had a feeling which he could hardly identify – that there was an exceptional detective in this man, one of very great potential which would develop only if he could control his impetuosity and his high opinion of himself.

At last, Moriarty said:

'I did when I first heard what had happened, sir, but it was soon apparent that it didn't really make much difference. We would have been told of the things found in the tank at Webb's, the Identi-kit picture would have been identified there, and we would have kept faith with Jill Hickersley. True there was no guarantee of it, but it's almost certain I did more harm than good.'

Roger sat down, more relieved than he cared to admit, and took out a bottle of whisky and two glasses. He placed these carefully on the blotting pad and went on much as if he were talking to his sons.

'You're going to make wrong decisions; we all are. Sometimes a wrong decision is going to make us hate ourselves. My experience is that decisions made in a hurry are more likely to be wrong than those made after reasonable consideration. It's also my experience that one officer, senior or junior, often makes a decision based on what he expects those working with him to do. There's more to discipline than a brainless toeing the line.' He paused. 'Scotch?'

'I'd like one very much, sir.'

Roger poured, and they drank. He had a feeling that there was something on Moriarty's mind. The other's whisky disappeared in three gulps.

'There's one other thing, sir.'

'Yes?'

'I – I'm an impatient devil.'

'So I've observed,' Roger said drily.

'I mean – rather more than that, sir. I *do* try to restrain myself. Impatience has been my problem for as long as I can remember. Other people sometimes seem so – so slow.'

'You mean you haven't learned to suffer those you consider to be fools, gladly,' Roger said. 'Another whisky?'

'Er – no, thanks. I'll soon be driving.'

Moriarty *and* Hilary Reed had that kind of conscience.

'I can tell you this,' said Roger. 'Your future at the Yard will depend on how well you succeed in mastering your impulses. I've seen a lot of top flight men finish no higher than Inspectors, disgruntled and serving out time for their pensions because they acted on impulse or hunch. Came precious close to it myself, once. Now!' He finished his drink and put his glass down. 'Send that special instruction out, then get off home. Let me know at Chelsea if you think anything's worth reporting.'

'Right, sir!' Moriarty was brisk, yet he hesitated. 'Have you seen the *Evening Globe*?'

'Yes.'

'You were behind that reward story, weren't you?' Something like admiration showed in the younger man's eyes.

'I knew it was on the way,' Roger said.

'Do you mind telling me what you expect from it?' Moriarty sounded almost humble.

'I don't expect anything,' Roger answered. 'I hope for a time when the next raid is coming off, and I wouldn't be surprised if we had a quiet night tonight and for several nights; we ought to have a chance to deal with the backlog of work.'

Moriarty said: 'I see, sir,' obviously not convinced, and went out.

Outside in the passage, Moriarty smiled sourly as he thought Well, I've calmed him down over that one, but he still thinks he knows the lot. He'll soon find out he's wrong.

Arriving home, Roger found Martin and Richard working in the garden with Janet, who looked hot and happy.

'Impeccably virtuous, though *not* entirely by choice, that's us,' Martin intoned with a grin.

'We've discovered that if you want to make a girl cool off you, the surest way at the moment is to invite her for a walk in the park,' Richard added.

'These boys are *impossible*!' protested Janet.

'You see, Dad, there was no such thing as sex in Mother's day,' Martin observed earnestly. 'Wasn't it clever of today's young people to discover it all by themselves?'

Over the commons and the parks, the open spaces and the secluded stretches of the Thames, there was a strange and unfamiliar quiet. The police, in uniform and plain clothes, were out in strength, and without exception they reported the same thing; very few couples were about. As dusk fell, all those who normally sought seclusion now appeared to avoid it. Here and there, a silent little drift of clinging couples still strolled on, until lost to sight; but most of them stayed within the radius of light. The pubs and cafés were full, as ribald jokes and lewd ones passed to and fro, bus and taxi drivers chatted unusually to their passengers, and wags demanded:

'*Any advance on one thousand quid?*'

The police, as alert as they had ever been, began to feel edgy by the time full darkness had fallen, listening for the screams and shouts which had broken the quiet on the previous night.

But none came. The night was still. And when pubs and cafés closed, the voices stilled and London slept.

Roger slept—

By half past seven he was up and making tea; by half past eight, fully refreshed and forgetful of his once painful shoulder, he was at the Yard. At once he became aware of an air of lightheartedness, even conviviality, blowing through the building. Seeking Moriarty, he found him with his jacket off, the sleeves of his shirt conspicuously white, filing the reports.

'Not a single attack!' he crowed.

'Hardly a single victim *to* attack,' a youthful, fresh-faced sergeant remarked. 'Talk about cleaning up London. Might be something in that idea after all, sir.'

'Just spray sulphuric acid and control the birth-rate,' chimed in another.

Roger said coldly: 'Teach them – don't make them.'

A man said irrepressibly: 'This'll larn 'em!'

They laughed lightheartedly, as they would have laughed at almost anything. Roger turned to the questionnaires, which were beginning to flood in. During the previous day, forty-seven young people had been charged with larceny – including shop-lifting, bag-snatching, pocket-picking; eleven had been charged with breaking and entering; seventeen with burglary; eleven with sexual offences including one multiple rape; nineteen with drunkenness; seventeen with causing malicious damage; a hundred and seven with some kind of car theft or driving offence.

'Average day,' Moriarty remarked.

'Yes,' agreed Roger. 'An average day. Now what I want to know is what crimes were committed between eight o'clock and midnight last night.'

'Any special reason, sir?'

'I'd like to know ,' Roger said evasively. By noon the figures were in; there had been fewer than usual crimes committed by young people during that period.

'*All* behaving themselves,' said Moriarty. 'Any news about Albert Young?'

'He stayed home. Alone. His wife stayed with relatives. What about his daughter?'

'She wasn't really well enough to talk, I couldn't get anything worthwhile out of her,' Moriarty said. 'Mind if I make a suggestion, sir?'

'Go ahead.'

'Will *you* see her?'

'Yes,' Roger said, after a moment's deliberation. 'This morning, I think. I'm going over to Putney, anyhow.'

The report on Albert Young was not particularly informative. He had for years been a leading social worker in a local church, but lately something not known had soured him. His daughter's reputation was neither better nor worse than average. She had had several boy-friends, and the night of the attack certainly hadn't been her first time out alone with one. 'Seems to know how to take care of herself,' one report read. Roger went from there to the house on Putney Hill, where Moriarty lived. It was a large, Victorian edifice, recently painted and fairly affluent looking, with trim lawns and well-kept shrubs. A maid answered the door, and soon he was in a downstairs room with a younger than middle-aged woman, well-preserved, attractive in a faintly antiseptic way; it would not have been surprising to find her as as a matron in a hospital.

'Mr Moriarty telephoned to say you might be calling,' she said, 'and Helena is up – she will be here in a few minutes. Will you forgive me for asking you to treat her as gently as you can, Superintendent?'

'It really wouldn't occur to me to do otherwise.'

'You're very kind,' the woman said formally.

A few minutes later, the girl came in. Her head was still bandaged, and she was paler than normal, but her eyes were clear and quite beautiful. The woman left them, and Roger found himself comparing this girl with little heart-faced Jill Hickersley. They had something in common – frankness of expression perhaps.

'The most important question I want to ask you is whether you ever knew a man named Clive Davidson,' Roger said, handing the girl a print taken from the photograph which Menzies had given him the previous night.

She glanced down, flushed, and said, 'Yes, I did.'

'Did you know him well?'

'We – we went out together quite a lot.'

'Why did the association cease?' Roger asked.

'My father disapproved. He frightened Clive off.'

'Frightened a young man like that? Do you know how he did it?'

'No, only – Clive stopped coming to see me.'

'Did your father frighten off any other of your admirers, Helena?'

She looked at him, troubled but quite frank.

'Yes.'

'Many?'

'Three. Three or four. Or maybe five.'

'Including Tony Wainwright?'

'He would have done, had he heard of it, but I hadn't known Tony for very long. Tony – Tony was going to marry me.'

Her father doubtless knew better than that, Roger reflected. Studying the girl, he believed that he could see the truth about her. She was what men like Wainwright – still in hospital and unable to lie on his back – would call a pushover. She was the kind from whom, when things went wrong, prostitutes were made. Even now in her eyes a seductive, 'bedroom' look glowed. She was exactly the type of girl he would not want his sons to bring home.

No doubt her father knew that, too.

'Helena,' Roger said, 'do you think your father capable of arranging an attack like the one on you?'

She didn't answer.

'Do you?' he insisted.

She said with sudden fire: 'In some moods he would do *anything*! It's always been the same, he *hates* it if my mother has a friend, a man friend. That's why he stopped going to church and doing the church work. Everyone liked *Mummy* but no one liked him. He couldn't bear it, so he stopped going and made her stop. He's horrible!'

'Has he ever used physical violence on you?'

'Often! Once he—' She caught her breath.

'Go on, Helena, please.'

'Once – once he threatened me with disfigurement; he said I was too pretty, that the only way to make a woman decent was to make her unattractive. Oh, I hate saying these things about my own father, but they're true, they really are. And he said he would *kill* any man who touched me or Mummy, and he meant it. He's a religious maniac, and absolutely crazy on the subject of sex! And now – now look what's happened! Who'll want to take *me* out when they realize the kind of things he'll do?'

'So you are afraid he attacked you and Tony,' Roger said flatly.

'Yes, I *am*!' she said. 'And his brother's just as bad.'

'His brother?'

'His half-brother really, his name's Delafield – Dick Delafield. They're both crazy and capable of anything. Daddy – Daddy terrifies men, and Uncle Dick tries to put them off women at that awful clinic. That's the truth – they're abnormal, they're *mad*.'

CHAPTER EIGHTEEN

NIGHT OF DECEPTION

'SHE IS lying,' Albert Young stated flatly.

'She is frightened, Mr Young.'

'She is frightened of her own wickedness.'

'Your wife did attempt suicide, sir.'

'My wife and my daughter share the same weakness of the flesh. My wife is—' Young hesitated, and then his face softened momentarily and he added less harshly: 'She is not able to control her weakness.'

He had nearly said: 'My wife is a whore.' There was suffering in this man's face, anguish in his eyes as he stood in the doorway of his shed. Behind him were the coils of rope, the chains, the anchors, the canvas, the drums of oil, the canned foods, the equipment for a ship's galley, everything a ship's chandler would stock; and the smell of oil, heavy on the air, reminded Roger vividly of Webb, Son, and King's factory. In this shop were weed-killers, garden tools, everything for the amateur gardener; and on a shelf only two yards away from Roger were two Amo spray guns.

'Mr Young,' Roger said, 'you have been known to utter threats against a number of men.'

'I have threatened them with the wrath of God!'

'You threatened to mutilate your daughter.'

'I have told you – that is a lie.'

'Why should she lie about you?'

'Because I prevented her from enjoying the fruits of her wickedness.'

Roger moved towards the oil store and the first thing to shock him was a carboy, parked in a straw-lined crate, with a label reading: CONCENTRATED SULPHURIC ACID. For Commercial Use. Manufactured by Webb, Son, and King.

'What is your opinion of the attacks being made on young couples, Mr Young? Do you see *those* as the wrath of God?'

Young said slowly: 'The Lord moves in mysterious ways.'

'Do you consider this to be one of the ways?'

'I am not fit to answer such a question. I can only pray for guidance and for a visitation upon the wicked.'

'Such as this acid-spraying?'

'Is it worse than the plague which strikes down evil-doers?'

'And strikes down the innocent, too,' retorted Roger.

Young almost spat out his next words. 'There are no innocents among these people! They are all wicked, as wicked as the people of Sodom and Gomorrah.'

Roger stared at him without expression for a long time. In a level voice, he asked: 'What do you use concentrated sulphuric acid for, Mr Young?'

Young said harshly: 'To burn away rusted metal, to rot hulls which cannot otherwise be destroyed. It is a cleansing as well as a burning agent. Did you not know that?' Young's eyes glistened with an anger he could not control. 'But I do not visit the wrath of the Lord on these sinners, I am not his chosen vessel. I bought that carboy of sulphuric acid for lawful purposes and it was brought to me by the man Davidson, who took advantage of my daughter's weakness of the flesh.'

'Did you murder him, Mr Young?'

Young looked astounded. 'Murder? Is the man *dead*?'

'He is missing, believed dead.'

'If he is dead it is the Lord's will,' said Young righteously. 'I know nothing of his death, but I do know there was no goodness in his life.'

Roger asked: 'When did you last go to Webb, Son, and King's factory?'

'I went there once, no more than that. The coward ran away.'

'So you frightened him, too, Mr Young.'

'Mr West,' said Young with sudden and unexpected dignity, 'you do not frighten me.'

'Watch him everywhere he goes,' Roger ordered the local police. 'It doesn't matter whether he discovers he's being watched or not; make sure we know every move he makes, if possible every telephone call he makes.'

'Superintendent,' said Young's ex-partner, Josephs, a big, nearly bald, priest-like man, 'I cannot help you. It is over a year since Mr Young stopped coming to church and doing the work which so needed doing. I seldom see him these days, except by chance.'

128

'Why did he stop his church work? Do you know?'

'There was a move to allow dancing at church socials, and he opposed it bitterly. His wife and daughter both supported it. He has always been a man of very intense feelings, Superintendent.'

'Does he have anything at all to do with the church social or youth club now?' asked Roger.

'Nothing, sir, nothing whatsoever,' Josephs answered, and the finality of his tone was yet a further indication of Young's adamance, his closed and prejudiced mind.

'The *Globe*'s had nothing in yet,' Pengelly said to Roger, 'except hundreds of letters of approval from our readers. The old man's positively purring.'

'So far, so good,' said Coppell, in a much more expansive mood. 'You're keeping something up your sleeve about this, Handsome, aren't you?'

'An idea, sir, that's all.'

'I know better than to ask you to share it,' the Commander said. 'But don't withhold any facts from me.'

'There's no trace of Clive Davidson,' Moriarty reported. 'It's beginning to look as if it was his body in the tank. We're trying to find his dentist so as to identify that bridge work and the tooth. If they're Davidson's—'

'Davidson himself could have thrown a man into the tank, and tossed his own dentures and watch in after him,' Roger pointed out. 'We're a long way from the truth yet. Did you have any luck with those footprints?'

'Footprints, sir – oh! Those from the factory. I asked Prints for a report, none's come through yet.'

'Ask them to get a move on,' Roger said. 'Three days is long enough even for Prints.'

'I'll fix it, sir. The nights are very quiet now,' Moriarty remarked. 'Three uneventful ones in a row, sir. Divisions say the bolder couples are beginning to creep back.'

'You know what, Dad? The girls like walking in the gloaming,' declared Richard.

'Roaming, clot!' said Martin.

129

'They're getting tired of going to the pictures every night,' Richard went on. 'Pity – *I* rather like it. All this necking business gets me down.'

'There is very little to report, sir,' Detective Constable Hilary Reed told Roger on the seventh day of her membership of Dr Lark's Club. 'Everything appears to be open and above board. Some of the films are a little suggestive, some of the literature is rather erotic, but my impression is that it *is* a genuine form of therapy, and that Dr Lark uses all the activities to find out what his patients are really like.'

'No amorous advances?'

The girl laughed. 'On the contrary, sir – I feel almost desexed.'

Roger was surprised into a chuckle.

'Don't let that happen! And don't take anything for granted. Think they suspect you?'

'I shouldn't think so for a moment.'

'What about the manager, Delafield?'

'He's a very good organizer, quiet and unobtrusive, and really the place is more like a clinic than a club.' Hilary Reed reported. 'Certainly they have two Amo sprays for fertilizing and spraying insects in the greenhouse, but no acid at all.' There was a note of disappointment in her voice. 'I have to admit that so far it's a blank.'

'What about the members, past and present?'

'The Australian, Wainwright, was one. Davidson was too – but that was in my written report.'

'Yes, I remember. Have you found out if Albert Young ever visits his half-brother?'

'Not yet, sir – I mean, I haven't found out. There is *one* thing—'

'What's that?'

'There's to be a very big party of past and present members here next Monday,' the girl told him. 'There's a big lecture room where, when the chairs are cleared away, there's space enough for over two hundred people to dance. It's to be fancy dress. I suppose this could be—' She broke off.

'An orgy?' suggested Roger.

'It seems absurd to suggest it on the knowledge I now have.'

'Nothing's absurd. Keep on being careful,' Roger advised.

And he thought how dreadful it would be if her lovely face was ever pocked from acid burns. At least she did not seem to be in the slightest degree perturbed, and he did not think she would take a single unnecessary risk.

'Mr Pengelly of the *Evening Globe* would like to see you sir.'

'*See* me. Is he *here*?'

'In the main hall, sir.'

'He knows the way – ask him to come along,' Roger said.

It was on a Saturday morning, ten days after the night of terror and after a period in which so little had happened that even the *Globe* had stopped putting the notice of the reward in its columns. Outside, rain smashed down against the window, beat on the big leaves of the plane trees, and splashed ankle high from the smooth surface of the roads. It was so overcast that all the lights were on and most cars and buses were lit up too.

Roger pushed aside the latest figures from the questionnaire. The comparative figures for the past month were now available, and there was little overall change. The information showed nothing of particular interest.

There was a tap at the door.

'Come in.' Roger stood up as Pengelly entered. 'To what do I owe—'

He broke off immediately, for obviously Pengelly had news. His eyes glowed, and he had a back-slapping look of rare exuberance.

'Hallo, Handsome! Give us a guess!'

'What have you got?' Roger almost held his breath.

'The break we've been waiting for,' Pengelly exclaimed. '*Three* squeaks, Handsome. *Three* claims for a reward.'

'Who from?' demanded Roger quickly.

'Anonymous informants who say they will establish their identity when they come to collect,' Pengelly said.

'Well, that's something. What's the squeak?'

'No less than that Monday is to be the big night!'

Roger had a flashing thought of another 'big night' on Monday, at the Lark Club.

'And all three informants say the same thing,' Pengelly continued, 'That there will be a bigger combined attack than ever on that evening – staggered, like the rest.'

'Well, well!' breathed Roger. 'So it might work.'

'But it's already worked!'

'Not yet,' said Roger, cautiously. 'We could slip up, and they could be fooling us. What kind of details did you get?'

Pengelly placed three neatly typewritten notes on the table, and Roger read one after the other in quick succession. They were all phrased differently but said exactly the same thing: Monday next was to be the biggest and most widespread attack staged yet on young couples in the open spaces in and near London. All three had come in by telephone and been received by Pengelly, who had typed out the notes himself.

'Hot from the earphones, Roger!'

Moriarty's excitement, when he heard the news, even beat Pengelly's. He tried to tone down his reaction after Pengelly had gone and he and Roger were together in Roger's office.

'They were bound to have another go soon, sir!'

'What do you make of the Monday Masked Ball at the Lark Club?' inquired Roger.

'Could be coincidence, but I don't see that it matters much. We'll have the club watched and all the rest of the Force concentrated on the commons and parks.' Moriarty scowled, as if suddenly realizing that there was uncertainty in Roger's manner. 'You can't doubt this information, sir.'

'Doubt it? It stinks,' Roger said roundly.

'*What?*'

'Don't tell Pengelly I said so – but *three* informants, all giving no names, all saying they'll identify themselves later, all within an hour of each other and giving precisely the same information. You aren't taken in by that, surely.'

Moriarty cried: 'But they must have been told *today*. They couldn't have given the information before they knew it.'

'*Three* of them,' repeated Roger. 'All after that one thousand pounds reward – all from the same gang.'

Moriarty said more calmly: 'You've almost got me guessing, now.' But he looked put out. 'What are you driving at, sir?'

'That we're being sold a pup,' Roger answered. 'We've been sold a pup all along. Listen to me, Inspector. These men are (*a*) Holy Joes or (*b*) hardened and brutal criminals. If Holy Joes, they're working out of conviction, and it's more than improbable that you would find *three* Judases among them. I

132

hardened criminals, then there must be a hell of a lot of loot to split up among a hundred or so of them, and one thousand wouldn't be enough to turn *three* into squealers, at the risk of acid-spraying in revenge. This, in my opinion, is an inspired "leak", to fool us.'

'*Fool us into what?*' cried Moriarty.

'Into watching the commons and parks on Monday night,' answered Roger, shortly.

'You mean you're not going to?' Moriarty almost squeaked.

'Not with all our men. *Listen!*' Roger repeated roughly. '*First*, we were forced to look at the Lark Club, by the spreading about – I could say *planting* – of those matches. *Second*, we were forced to look at Albert Young – in fact we got to him later than we should have done. *Third*, Clive Davidson was marked down as a victim, but was the only one who suffered a very bad jolt, without serious injury. It was obviously a warning, and it frightened him away. Every move so far has had the one definite purpose – to make us look in the wrong place. Even Webb, Son, and King's may be a false trail.'

'Then what's the real one?' demanded Moriarty.

'If I knew that, I'd be on to it by now,' Roger said. 'The certain thing is, there *is* one. And the next nearest to a certain thing is that these men are *not* Holy Joes. You might get a group of honest fanatics sit in on one big wrath-of-God act but you wouldn't get a lot of them creeping out at night and squirting acid. This is a big criminal plot, don't make any mistake about it.'

Moriarty said: 'You've almost got me convinced, sir.'

Roger stared at him and said nothing.

He's mad, Moriarty thought, he's absolutely crazy!

'Well,' conceded Commander Coppell, after Roger had reported to him, 'you're probably right, and you'd better work on that assumption. What do you want to do?'

'Have one third of the Force in the parks and on the commons on Monday, one third on the usual beats and—' Roger broke off. 'No, sir,' he went on at last. 'One third in the parks and on the commons, one third in reserve in the Divisions to move in if the trouble does break out there, one third standing by for emergency work elsewhere – with a good Force available for the Lark Club, for safety's sake.'

'You're talking about the on-duty forces, I gather,' Coppell said.

'No, sir. I'm talking about one hundred per cent. I think all leave should be cancelled for Monday night, and every man we've got should be on duty.'

'But that'll cost a fortune in overtime!'

'If we don't make a thorough job of it, the consequences could be even more expensive,' Roger argued.

'I'd better see what I can do.' Coppell was not pleased, but prepared to give way. 'I'll talk to the Assistant Commissioner first thing on Monday morning. He's away for the weekend.'

That would give time – just time – provided the Assistant Commissioner didn't dither too long. Roger spent an edgy weekend at home, devoting a lot of concentration to reading the Sunday newspapers' 'theories' about the attacks, and sundry sultry warnings about the calm before the storm. Then he drafted his request to the Divisions and Headquarters Force.

All leave and off-duty hours stopped from Monday, 4 p.m.
$33\frac{1}{3}$ per cent of all Divisional and HQ forces in parks and commons.
$33\frac{1}{3}$ per cent in reserve for immediate move to parks and commons.
$33\frac{1}{3}$ per cent in reserve for other emergencies including a force of 25 men within easy reach of the Lark Club.

At eight-thirty on Monday morning he was in his office. At nine, Coppell came in. At half past nine, Coppell went to see the Assistant Commissioner. At nine forty-five, when Moriarty was in Roger's office, Roger's internal telephone bell rang.

'Go ahead,' Coppell said. 'Send the instruction out.'

'Go ahead!' Roger cried to Moriarty. 'Get it out. Don't lose a minute.'

Moriarty left the office smartly, but as the door closed on him, his face darkened and he muttered: 'It's crazy, absolutely crazy. Every man we've got ought to be in the parks and on the commons. West is *wrong*.'

Then it dawned on him that he had it in his power to put West right – *he* could alter the percentages, and once the instructions were out, it would be too late to countermand them. His eyes began to burn.

CHAPTER NINETEEN

MORIARTY'S DECISION

MORIARTY went along to his office, tight-lipped, angry, bitter. He felt instinctively that Superintendent West was wrong. Hadn't he himself admitted that he was as liable to mistakes as the next man? And his reasoning was certainly at fault. Holy Joes weren't proof against money-making – my God! He knew plenty of churchgoers who paid more homage to hard cash than anything 'spiritual'. It was obvious that they were fighting an organization of fanatics – who else would do the crazy things these people had done?

Ordinary criminals wouldn't; he, Moriarty, knew too many of them too well. They wouldn't spray acid over couples anywhere, their sympathy would be with the couples – with the men, anyhow. They might spray good luck, but acid – the very idea was crazy!

Albert Young was a typical Holy Joe. He might not be involved in this but – look what he had done to his own daughter and to his wife. The Lark Club might be the real cover, who knew? As for Clive Davidson, plenty of people had the guts and the motive to push him into an acid bath.

West was *wrong*. This was a Holy Joe campaign by a lot of fanatical young fools, and they were going to stage a massive attack on Monday. Everyone ought to be at action stations – at parks and commons, everywhere the attacks had been staged before. The only thing right about this special instruction was cancelling leave and off-duty for the night.

Two sergeants were in the office, and one asked:

'Any news?'

Moriarty grunted: 'No.'

The sergeant shrugged; almost at once Moriarty's telephone bell rang. He lifted it sharply:

'Detective Inspector Moriarty here.'

'Superintendent West,' Roger West said. 'I've just been called to a conference at the Home Office, so that leaves it to you to get everything under way and handle emergencies yourself. If you need extra help, discuss it with Superintendent Peel.'

'Right, sir!'

West rang off. Moriarty sat at his desk feeling a surge of excitement as he pored over the situation. One third, parks and commons, one third reserve, ditto, one third to meet unnamed emergencies – there wouldn't be any emergencies, just the usual crop of crimes. Anyhow, what difference would it make if a few old lags got away with a haul or two tonight? *Half* in parks and commons, *half* on reserve, that was more like it.

Moriarty realized that the sergeants were looking at him oddly.

He snatched up the instruction, and crossed to the maps on the wall.

The truth was, there should be a different approach altogether. Take the danger areas and have one third in them, well hidden during daylight; have one third in a mobile cordon, to move in after dark, after the attackers had got through, then have the remaining third of the Force in reserve to go anywhere they were wanted. He selected Hyde Park and Wimbledon Common, ringed them round with a sweeping arc in blue, then a wider arc in green, then placed the reserves at key points marked X. He knew exactly how the Divisions would work. All they needed was the go-ahead.

This – *this* idea was what they would expect, too; no one would be surprised.

He moved back to his desk, picked up the receiver and said: 'Commander's office.' The sergeants raised their eyebrows. 'Commander's secretary ... Do you know if he had gone to the Home Office Conference with Mr West ... What time do you expect him back, please? ... Not until then?' His voice rose. 'Thank you.'

He rang off.

West couldn't find out what had been done until late this afternoon!

Supposing he, Moriarty, did change the order? In the long run, who would benefit? West, of course. And it couldn't go wrong; Moriarty was quite sure of that. If West tore a strip off him, what of it? He'd soften up pretty quickly once he'd seen the *results* from Moriarty's better judgement. He pretended to be tough but he was like putty. It wouldn't be beyond him to take all the credit.

Moriarty almost cried out in indignant protest.

He sat down and drew a diagram of what he proposed, taking special care. Then he took it along to the office for copying – it wasn't a thing which could go out on teletype, but copies could reach every divisional station within two hours. Ah! Moriarty's eyes glistened. If he sent the 'Cancel leave and off-duty from 4 p.m.' and signed it as by West for Coppell, the Divisions would act on that at once, it wouldn't matter if they received details an hour or two later; in fact the later the better. There was plenty of time.

At ten o'clock, the teletype instruction about leave was sent.

By twelve noon, all the photo-copies of the detailed instructions were on their way to Divisions with a letter to Kensington to hold a dozen men in reserve for the Lark Club; the Yard could supply the rest.

So it was done.

'He'll be bloody glad he left me in charge,' Moriarty said.

After lunch, the sergeants noticed that he had a high colour and had been drinking too heavily. They wondered what Handsome West would say if he knew; West was the last man to approve of Dutch courage. Moriarty was at his desk when a call came, and at first he took it casually.

'Yes, Mrs Reed?' It was Hilary's mother, who often called with messages. 'What's that ... Er – yes. Yes, that's right, it's a big day. No need to worry.' He rang off, wiped his forehead, and looked up at the sergeants. 'Detective Constable Reed hasn't been in, has she?'

'Not to my knowledge,' one man answered.

'She's been missing from home all day,' Moriarty said. 'What the hell do I do now?'

'Wait for Handsome, he knows the answers!'

Moriarty sprang to his feet, and roared: 'Who the hell do you think you're talking to? I know the answers a bloody sight better than West. He's on his way out, any damned half-wit could see that.'

He stormed out of the office.

'If you ask me, Mr Inspector-so-and-so-Moriarty is heading for the high jump,' one sergeant remarked.

'If you ask me, Hilary Reed's in trouble,' said the other worriedly. 'What do you think we ought to do about it?'

Hilary Reed had put down the telephone after talking to Roger West, smiling faintly at his repeated warnings. West had a paternal manner with her, but unlike Paddy Moriarty, she rather liked it. The serenity at the Lark Club had at first puzzled, and then made her suspicious, but now she took it for granted. Most of her work was routine. She did not seriously expect to find out anything startling, and after Monday's Masked Ball she would almost certainly be assigned to another job. 'Do-gooding' didn't appeal as much as she had expected to; in a perverse way, her perverted but pathetic old men seemed to be in more need of attention.

On that Sunday morning she had left the St John's Wood flat without thinking of danger. It was only her second Sunday at the Club but she knew there would be religious services for those who wanted them, for in a rather unusual way the atmosphere at the Lark Club was undoubtedly churchy. She had made up and dressed in her best, and was well aware of the admiring glances cast in her direction as she travelled from her flat in St John's Wood to the Club. Turning into the wide entrance, she found Dr Lark and Delafield lingering in the hall.

'Good morning, Miss Reed!' Lark's voice was almost playful. 'How very charming you look. I'll wager no one would think you were attending a psychiatric clinic.'

'You see how much good you've done me already,' she replied.

'I like to think so. I do indeed.' Lark took her arm, the first even half-familiar gesture he had made. 'Mr Delafield and I have some special interviews this morning, I wonder if you would sit in for him.'

'Of course.'

'If there are any telephone calls, simply take the messages,' Lark said. 'And in emergency my receptionist will know where to find me.'

It seemed so friendly and above board that there was no thing at all to arouse Hilary's suspicions. When she got into the secretary's office, she realized the extent of her opportunity. No one else was in on Sunday morning, she could make a thorough search for records of the men and women whom West believed might once have been members. She put a wastepaper basket by the door, so that she would have warning of anyone's approach, and ran through the file marked: Ex-Members. In most of the folders there were photographs, and all of them were of strangers, except one of Anthony Wainwright, the Australian. The few details about him included his job, but nothing the Yard did not know already.

She heard a creak outside, and sprang back from the filing cabinet; but it was a false alarm.

Then she found a card for a Clive Davidson – in a file at the back of the others, and out of alphabetical order. For the first time, her heart began to beat faster and hopefully. There were other folders here. She glanced through one and saw *Menzies, M. C.* – the manager at Webb, Son, and King; she had never seen him but Moriarty had described him well, with his fleshy features and heavy jowl.

She opened the next folder – and had one of the shocks of her life.

Here was the photograph of a man who had been in prison several times, one of the youngest 'old lags' known to the Yard; and the next three in this special section were all professional criminals, expert safe-breakers, and burglars. Now her heart was beating very fast indeed; almost choking her.

Next she saw a list of names and addresses in Delafield's writing, and in front of it a note saying: To report on Monday – after the Masked Ball begins.

Why should these confirmed criminals report here?

She did not know and could not really guess; all she knew was that she must report this to West or Moriarty, at once. She daren't risk using this telephone but once Delafield came back she could go to the nearest call-box. She put all the files back in position, and went to the door, impatient now to leave the club.

Standing just outside the door was Delafield, so much a younger edition of Albert Young.

Standing by his side was Josiah Lark.

In Delafield's hand was an Amo spray gun.

Shocked, Hilary stood absolutely still. Neither man spoke. After the first moment, she began to reason. They were at the head of the stairs, and she had only to get past them to get down to the hall. Delafield wasn't very strong and she knew more about in-fighting and judo than these two put together;

139

the only danger was from that spray gun, but if she kicked i
aside. . . .

Two men appeared at the foot of the stairs.

'My dear Miss Reed, I shouldn't attempt to escape,' Lar
said in the now familiar playful voice. 'We just want to as
you a few questions, that's all.'

'What – what is Mr Delafield doing with that spray gun?'

'Waiting to use it,' Delafield said. 'Go back into the office
She hesitated.

Delafield touched the trigger of the gun, and terror sho
through Hilary. A few spots of liquid fell on her skirt. Sh
glanced down and saw holes appear in the material almost a
once. Slowly, eyes enormous as she stared from the gun t
Lark and back to Delafield, she retreated into the office.

'Who *are* you?' demanded Lark.

'You – you know—' she moistened her lips. 'You know ver
well who I am.'

'I shouldn't answer evasively,' Lark said. 'Mr Delafiel
really enjoys using the gun. And you have such a nice com
plexion.'

Her tongue seemed to cleave to the roof of her mouth.

'I – I am a police officer, And I warn you—'

Delafield said in a mocking voice: 'Anything you say ma
be used in evidence – for or against you.' He drew nearer an
pushed her towards a chair. She dropped into it, fightin
panic. 'Now, how much have you told the police?'

'Nothing!'

'Delafield,' Lark said, 'if we raise her skirt a few inches
that stretch of leg above the stocking, and you just spra
lightly there, the acid will soon begin to burn. She won't l
disfigured enough to matter, but she will know we're i
earnest.' He moved forward, and actually put a hand on he
skirt where holes now gaped. 'Miss Reed – what *have* you tol
your superiors?'

Hilary gasped: 'How could I tell them anything? – yo
fooled me. They know about the dance, but does that matter
The dreadful spray gun was only inches from her face.

'What did you have to find out?'

'Anything I could of course. I had to try to identify certai
people as members, I—'

'What people?'

140

'A – a few of the victims of – of the acid.' She drew further back from the spray, her breathing laboured.

'There were . . .'

She gave the names, still fighting for breath, and as she did so she hated herself because she was so afraid. She had one gleam of comfort – just one. Roger West's insistence that she shouldn't make a heroine of herself.

At last, they seemed satisfied that she had told them everything.

'Now you will be our guest for a day or two, though not here, naturally. You will be able to help us on Monday, Miss Reed.' Lark was positively unctuous. 'If your friends send spies to the Ball you will be able to identify them for us.'

Delafield held out two tablets.

'Take these,' he said. 'They'll send you to sleep.'

'No. I refuse to take—'

'Or would you rather have the needle?' Delafield demanded roughly.

She took the tablets, by no means sure whether she would ever wake from the sleep they would induce. She began to doze off within minutes of taking them, her last waking thoughts being: *What a heroine, what a heroine, what a heroine.*

That was while Roger was in his conference, and Moriarty was fuming and rebellious, at the office; and before the final decision had been made about what the police should do on Monday night.

CHAPTER TWENTY

MONDAY NIGHT

At half past four, Roger left the Home Office with Coppell. They sat at the back of a big black limousine and were driven a quarter of a mile to Scotland Yard. Roger was very much on edge and would rather have walked. It was a warm afternoon, the sun still high, the kind of afternoon which normally preceded crowded open spaces and a perfect setting for young love. He had sat through most of the day of highly specialized discussion, not quite sure that he knew what the Home Office wanted.

'They think we should be a Preventive Force,' Coppell said, in a tone of disgust. 'I know one thing, Handsome, we're going to fight such nonsense. When a crime's committed, and only then, we can step in. We're not a welfare society.'

'I know what you mean,' Roger said.

In one way he agreed with Coppell, in another he didn't, but one thing was certain. He and his questionnaire had been used by Coppell and the VIPs at the Yard as an effort to satisfy the Home Office that the police were doing all that was practicable to find motives and to seek means of preventing crime. It hadn't been successful. The Home Office wanted the Yard to do more, and from now on the Yard was going to argue that Welfare and Social Service work were not their responsibilities. The argument might go on for weeks; even months. He was to continue along the lines he had started, but Coppell had made one thing clear at the conference.

'When a job comes along like this acid spraying, the investigation has to take precedence over the other work. That's essential.'

No one had argued.

'Got the human aspect of the acid job on your mind, haven't you?' Coppell remarked with unexpected perception.

The incredible thing, however, was that he, Coppell, hadn't.

They parted at the top of the main steps, Roger to turn into his own empty office. There was a note from Moriarty but no copies of the instructions which had been sent out. Roger rifled through the papers to make sure of this, then read the note.

10.15 a.m. Detective Constable Hilary Reed has been missing since yesterday (Sunday) morning. Have reassured her mother. What action recommended, please.

Roger thought, shocked: They must've discovered who she is. And then, wryly: At least Moriarty's coming to me for advice.

It was seven hours since this note had been left. He rang for Moriarty as he went through the other papers, mostly questionnaires. A number of his old friends on the Force had written pungent notes: 'Welfare Officer now, Handsome?' And: 'Don't you think we've enough to do?' And: 'Going in for politics?' And: 'No wonder the little darlings are spraying acid.' Normally these would have amused him, but where the hell was Moriarty?

There was a tap at the door and Moriarty came in; he was very red-faced and his eyes had blood-streaks; Roger thought: he's drunk, and then: He can't be. Just scared now that we've come to the crisis. He checked the harshness in his voice.

'What have you done about Detective Constable Reed?'

'Nothing.'

'Nothing?' Roger was startled. 'Good God, man—'

'If I had, Bell – Mr Bell would have ordered a search of the Lark Club. They wouldn't have kept her there and it would have given too much away. So I waited for *you* to decide.'

Roger thought: here's real trouble. But it was upwards of six o'clock, he needed a meal, then needed to check that everything was set by dusk; he could deal with Moriarty tomorrow.

'Send two men over, tell the Lark Club we're looking for a *Miss* Hilary Reed, who may be able to give us some help.' Roger broke off, and his tone changed. 'I'll send 'em, you go back to the Operations Room. Is everything set?'

'Everything's set,' said Moriarty.

'Be at the ready,' ordered Roger.

He's a pushover!' breathed Moriarty, outside the door. *'He's easy. Tomorrow he'll be thanking me.* Now who ought to be the boss?'

By seven o'clock, a report came in that Hilary Reed had been to the Lark Club on Sunday morning and had left before lunch. Lark himself and the club secretary both said this.

Could she have decided to do a lone wolf act? wondered Roger. And he thought: I'm beginning not to understand these youngsters at all. He went to the canteen for a meal, was tapped on the shoulder by a Superintendent who asked:

'All ready for the big night, Handsome?'

'All ready.'

'Wish you luck.'

'I need it.' Roger went back to his office and checked with four key divisions, Central London, Wimbledon, Dulwich, and Hampstead. He used the same phraseology each time, not dreaming how much it could conceal. 'All set for tonight? . . .

143

You'll follow instructions to the letter, won't you? ... The reserves at the ready? ... Good, thanks.'

At half past eight, with an hour still to go before dusk, he walked along to the Operations Room, where Moriarty was waiting with the two sergeants.

'Both of you sergeants go to Hampstead,' he ordered. 'Moriarty, get out to Wimbledon at once, will you?'

'Right.' Moriarty seemed delighted, although Roger had expected him to want to stay at the heart of the investigation here at the Yard where the reports would start coming. But he did not leave until Roger had gone out, and when he went he took his files with him. Still completely oblivious of the real state of affairs, Roger went down to the Information Room. Reports were coming in already.

'First men in position,' said Division after Division.

'Be a mess if someone chooses tonight to start a mass raid in town,' the Information Room Inspector said.

'That's what I'm ready for,' said Roger.

'It's what you're what?' The other man, tall and lanky, had a habit of swallowing his words. Roger hardly heard him but checked that both Webb, Son, and King, and the Lark Club were surrounded. The Information Room Inspector came up to him along the line of uniformed men who were reading teletype messages which were coming through in a constant clatter of noise, and telephone messages from telephones which never seemed to stay silent.

'*Hyde Park back to normal.*'

'*Kensington Gardens – normal amount of couples around.*'

'*Wimbledon Common – you'd think no one had heard of acid.*'

'*Hampstead Heath – at least two hundred couples bedded down already.*'

'Mr West.'

'Yes?'

'What did you say?'

'About what?'

'Being ready for a lot of raids in the metropolitan area.'

'I am. That's what the reserve's for.'

'What?' The man looked blank.

'What do you think they're for?' demanded Roger impatiently.

144

'But – they're at the commons and parks.'

'What on earth are you talking about?'

'They are – look, if you don't believe me. They moved in support. That's what *you* ordered.' He picked up one of the copies of Moriarty's instructions. 'Couldn't be clearer than that.'

Roger stared down, beginning to read. As he did so, a tight band seemed to clutch at his chest and ice to harden in his veins. It was some seconds before he could relax, aware of the puzzled gaze of the Inspector. When he moistened his lips, they were stiff; when he spoke, it actually hurt the back of this throat.

'Put out a call for Moriarty,' he grated. 'I want him here, at once, and—'

He broke off as a constable came up with a teletype note in his hand.

Collinsons of Hatton Garden raided – guards sprayed with acid. Loss not yet known.

'Look at that!' gasped the Information Room Inspector.

All over London, the raids were taking place. Except for a few uniformed men on the beat, and some on traffic duty in the theatre district, the heart and suburbs of London were denuded of police, and the Flying Squad cars and the patrol cars were all concentrated on the open spaces. With swift, ruthless efficiency, jewellers' shops, safe deposits and wholesale diamond merchants were raided; in Hatton Garden only two firms of any consequence escaped. The big stores were burgled methodically and their jewel departments ransacked. Jewellery which had been stored in safe deposits for years was taken. Museums and galleries were broken into with calm effrontery; dynamite and nitroglycerine were used without any serious attempt to drown the noise.

Oxy-acetylene burners were used by the dozen, steel bars, steel doors and intricate locks were burned out, and the loot was taken. All over London the burglar alarms sounded, all over London horrified night-watchmen and security men telephoned the police, requests for help flooded the Divisions as well as the City of London police and New Scotland Yard – and only here and there could help be sent, for the whole of London's Police Force was concentrated on the open stretches,

the parks and commons and the riverside – where the young
lovers found their dreams of ecstasy, and lost them without
any interference from the acid-sprayers, and while the police
waited in exasperation.

At last, urgent calls came for them to go back to their Division, but by then it was too late.

A hundred burglaries had taken place within forty-five minutes. So far no one could begin to reckon the cost, but one
Hatton Garden merchant talked in despair of a consignment
worth nearly a million pounds.

Two watchmen were killed.

Twenty-seven were injured, eleven burned with acid.

Only one man was caught, because he slipped down some
stairs and sprained his ankle.

Word came through almost as he finished the reports, saying
that the party at the Lark Club was in full swing.

'We'll raid the place with thirty men,' Roger decided.

He led the raid himself, when the Masked Ball was at its
height; nothing could have been more innocuous. Lark was
there as a Harlequin, easily recognizable although masked.

'I do assure you, Superintendent, this club is *most* reputable. If you insist on having all the revellers unmasked, of
course, I will arrange it.'

In fact, no one semed to mind.

'And you may have my keys and roam anywhere you like,'
Lark said. 'My house, like my heart, is an open book.'

The police found nothing at all of interest at the club or in
the clinic. It was as much a failure as the rest of the police
operations had been – a bitter anti-climax.

Roger studied the summary of the night's reports with a bleak-
ness he had never experienced before. He had a sense of utter
failure and a surging bitterness because Moriarty had defied
him – another man was responsible for his, Roger's, abysmal
failure. Moriarty was on the way from Wimbledon; Roger was
in his office when his telephone bell rang.

'West.'

'This is Commander Coppell.' Coppell's voice was harsh,
angry. 'What's been going on, West?'

Roger said: 'However bad you think it is, sir, it's worse.'

'But this is catastrophic! I thought you – wait there – I'll come at once.'

Coppell rang off, and Roger lowered his receiver. The bell rang and he hesitated for a moment before picking it up.

'West.'

'There are a dozen newspapermen at the Back Room, we've got to give them a statement soon,' the Back Room Inspector said.

'Later.'

The bell rang again.

'West ... *What!* Are you sure? ... Yes, bring him to my office, at once.' Roger put the receiver down with the first lift of heart he had known since realizing what had happened. He lit a cigarette, and was staring out of the window when the prisoner was carried in. He was a little man with very lean, hard features, and the sly yet defiant look of an old hand.

'Blimey,' he said, 'Handsome West hisself – this is an honour, Handsome!'

Roger said: 'You were caught with acid and a spray gun – don't think there's anything funny in this. Where were you going to take the loot?'

'Loot – what loot? I was just taking a walk for the sake of me health.'

'Lay off the funny stuff,' Roger ordered. 'Where were you going to take the loot?'

'Tell you what,' the thief said earnestly, 'you've had a rough night, so I'll give you a break. I was to telephone the Man on the Moon, and *he* was to gimme the instructions.'

It would be a waste of time to question him any more. Roger sat at his desk, profoundly troubled, and ran through the reports he hadn't yet seen. One which caught his eye carried copies of two footprints showing points of similarity which proved they had been made by the same boot or shoe.

One had been found on Wimbledon Common, after an acid attack; the other at Webb, Son, and King's factory.

At least that was a point for Moriarty ...

Coppell looked an old man as he sat at Roger's desk; old and crushed.

'Can't you *make* the prisoner talk, West?'

'No, sir. And I don't think he ever will. He knows he and his family will be well looked after if he keeps quiet, but be sprayed with acid if he doesn't. Even if we pick up the others the pattern will be the same. There's just one thing puzzling me—'

'There's a hell of a lot puzzling *me*. Why didn't you send out the orders as I approved? What went wrong?'

'I don't know yet, sir,' Roger said stonily.

'Well, *I* want to know at once.'

Nearby, Moriarty was waiting; he could be called in now he could be blamed, he could – he would – be suspended forthwith and he would be dismissed from the Force. None of this altered the fact that he, Roger, had failed to send the instructions out personally, had left such a vital task to a subordinate. At the time, it had seemed more than sufficient for him to prepare the general instructions; it had never entered his head that Moriarty would change so much as a word. He could not, he did not blame himself; but he would never be able to evade the responsibility for what had happened.

'The thing which puzzles me is the fact that *only* jewellery has been stolen,' he said flatly. 'There's been a few odd thousands of pounds in notes, but banks were raided for jewellery in their safe deposits, not for money – millions of pounds have been passed over.'

'What's so remarkable?' Coppell demanded. 'Money's easy to trace, but diamonds aren't.'

'They're difficult to sell and difficult to hide. They—'

Roger broke off, and even Coppell, angry though he was, was silenced by the expression in his eyes, the change in his whole manner. It was almost as if Roger had suddenly found a fortune.

At last, Coppell said: 'What's on your mind?'

In a strained voice, Roger said: 'The hiding place. A place where diamonds can be hidden with practically no chance of being found. The place which is open by night and where a night shift begins at midnight. The place where we found a footprint identical with one found at the scene of one of the assaults.'

'You mean that chemical factory?' Coppell said, frowning.

'I mean Webb, Son, and King's,' answered Roger tensely 'A tiny diamond found in the sludge was believed to be from

148

Davidson's signet ring. It was undamaged. But it's going to be a hellish place to raid, sir.'

Outside his office, Moriarty was standing with two detective sergeants. As Roger and Coppell went out, there was a look of piteous entreaty on the young detective's face. Coppell was too preoccupied to pay much attention. Roger said:

'Excuse me, sir.'

Coppell went on, Roger went ahead of Moriarty into his own office. The once handsome face had lost all its attractiveness, the strong hands shook. Roger stared at him for a long time, until Moriarty burst out:

'I would rather have killed myself than let this happen!'

Roger thought: He *might* kill himself, too.

He thought: Ought I to let him go home and give him the chance?

Harshly, angrily, he said: 'I'm going to put you on a charge. That means you'll be in the cells at Cannon Row overnight. I'll see you in the morning.'

He left the man and went up to the Laboratory, his mind quite set on what he was going to do. If this sensational raid was wholly successful, if the thieves got away with their haul, then the Yard would be a laughing stock and he would be the grandaddy of the joke against the whole Metropolitan Police Force. It was not simply that he would never live it down, or that it would undo practically all the good effect of his twenty-odd years of effort, of sacrifice, of dedication. It was the fact that he – that *he* would have let the yard down; and let the public down. There might be one way of avoiding it: to find the jewels and capture the criminals.

And he would have to do this himself.

He went into the empty Laboratory, found and pulled on a pair of plastic gloves, then picked up the Amo spray gun which had been recently tested. Handling it very cautiously, he checked that there was some acid still in it. Against one wall was a baby's shawl, a pair of stockings, and a handkerchief. He squeezed the Amo trigger. A fine spray of the acid hissed out, the nylon began to crinkle at once and when he pulled it, it tore easily. After a few seconds, the handkerchief rotted too, and soon the woollen shawl began to peel apart. This was concentrated sulphuric acid beyond doubt.

He went down to Fingerprints, which was as empty as the Laboratory, everyone, he thought bitterly, being on special duty. He had noticed earlier a small zipper bag, among the discarded articles. He placed the Amo gun inside it, zipped and unzipped the fastening, making sure he could get at the gun easily. Then he went out.

CHAPTER TWENTY-ONE

THE HIDING PLACE

YES, Roger thought, it's a hell of a place to raid.

He stood on a roof, a few streets away from the factory, seeing the fire from one of the ovens, remembering everything he had seen there. He was waiting for word, now, that two cordons of police, carrying plastic gloves and masks, were in position. If the thieves panicked they might make a concerted rush, spraying acid at random, and there were limits to what the police could risk.

His walkie-talkie radio buzzed.

'Everything's ready, sir.'

'Right.' Roger started down a ladder. 'Order the men to put on masks and gloves at the slightest sign of danger.'

'Yes, sir. Many of them have also been equipped with protective suits.' The man at the other end of the radio was waiting on the cobbled street, and as Roger stepped alongside him he went on: 'May I suggest that you yourself wear one before going in, sir.'

'Impossible. If I did, they'd know at once we were going to raid them,' Roger said decisively. 'That's the last thing I want.'

'It's a very big risk, sir.'

'Could well be,' (but so was Hilary Reed's) 'nevertheless it's one that has to be taken. I'm going alone, for a start. If I'm not out in ten minutes, send for me. If the necessity arises, give orders for the raid to begin.'

As he approached the Works Entrance of the factory he thought of the sediment and the human sludge he had seen here on his first visit and of the calm, distinguished beauty of

Hilary Reed. The harsh fact was that she might have been thrown into the acid.

His mind revolted against the thought, refusing to accept it.

No one was in the narrow, bleak entrance passage. On two walls were two time-stamping machines, and racks upon racks of time cards. One rack was headed: Night Shift. He made a swift calculation; there were about a hundred men on the night shift and there had been about a hundred jewel raids. What simpler than to bring the stolen diamonds here, with the gold, silver, and platinum of the settings and toss the jewels into an acid which would not harm them but with which only experts would work? He stepped out of the passage into the main part of the factory. Twenty or thirty men were working behind the rails in special suits and masks. At one bench a muffled figure was sitting on a high stool, rather like an umpire at a tennis match. A man came up to Roger.

'Help you?'

'Is Mr Menzies in?'

'Who shall I say?'

'West.'

'Just West?'

'Superintendent West of the CID,' replied Roger, showing his card.

The man said in a startled voice: 'A copper!'

'That's right,' Roger said coldly. 'Get a move on. I haven't got all night.'

He waited, alert to everything that followed. The man who had accosted him said nothing more but gestured to others, who moved towards the door behind Roger, swiftly covering all exits. Some would go outside, to see who else was there; they would see his empty car. They might go further afield and see the police cars, but that would not necessarily prevent him from doing what he had set out to do.

Man after man turned his head, levelling at him stares both insolent and furtive. Two men went up the open stairs to the platform, approaching the figure who was sitting there. No one was working at this tank, though each of the others had been approached.

Fear slashed at Roger. Could that be because of Hilary Reed?

He heard a man approaching and would have recognized

him by his heavy breathing; Menzies. Roger turned.

'What's on?' demanded Menzies.

Roger unzipped his bag.

'I want some help with this,' he said, and put his hand round the gun. He did not draw it out or show what it was, but went on in the same even voice. 'And first I want Detective Constable Reed, here by my side.'

Menzies caught his breath.

'*Whaaat!*'

'You heard me.'

'You're crazy!'

'I'm much saner than you are, I assure you,' Roger said amiably. 'I don't, for instance, think I can get away with the impossible. And when I've got her, I want the diamonds.'

'. . . crazy!' Menzies rasped, and raised his right hand.

At the manhole next to the one where Hilary might be, there was a sudden flurry of movement followed by a sight Roger had never thought to see: a sudden shimmering cascade of brilliant, many-hued light. Like a liquid rainbow it spilled from a bucket in a man's hand into the acid which was out of Roger's sight. It was over in a second, a fleeting waterfall of scintillating brilliance; and when it was gone, the whole room seemed to be darkened.

'We haven't got any diamonds,' Menzies said.

'You really want to take the rap for Lark, don't you?'

'I don't know what you're talking about.'

Two men approached the 'umpire'. Both of them wore protective uniforms and hoods. They reached either side of the high stool, then one of the men put a hand to the 'umpire's' neck.

A door opened and a little man with a cherub's face came in; there was an expression of sheer malevolence in his pale blue eyes.

'We're surrounded,' he stated, and glared at West.

'Just bring the girl and get the jewels back,' Roger ordered, blandly.

'What's in the bag?' demanded Menzies, but before Roger could answer he said to the little man: 'Go tell Lark.'

Roger said: 'Telling Lark won't help. Nothing will help you now.'

Oaths ripped through the air.

'Listen,' said Menzies, 'nothing helps anybody who falls into that acid.'

'Then see that nobody else falls into it.'

'Listen,' Menzies said again, and wiped the sweat from his red neck. 'You've got a radio in that bag. Use it. Tell your men outside to get away from here and let us out. Or – *you'll* go into the vat. *After she's in.*'

It must have been a coincidence, but a man by the 'umpire' pushed a hood off the seated person's head; and the fair shining hair was Hilary Reed's. As it settled, almost to her shoulders, she stared at Roger. It was possible to believe that he could see the terror in her eyes.

No one was working now; hardly a person moved, except to take off the shiny plastic suits and move slowly towards the exits. Obviously everything had been planned to the last detail, even what to do in a police raid.

'You heard me!' Menzies rasped. 'Tell your men to back off!'

Slowly, deliberately, Roger drew the Amo gun out of the bag. Too late to prevent Roger from backing a pace and pointing it at his blotchy red face, Menzies realized what he held. As if they all saw it at the same moment, the men stopped moving. There was a hiss of breath, as if everyone had breathed in at the same moment.

Roger said: 'If you don't want this concentrated sulphuric acid in your face, Menzies, you'll do what you're told.' He saw the ugly jaw drop open, the yellow teeth exposed in an uneven line. 'Bring the woman here.'

Menzies said chokily: 'They – they won't bring her!'

'Then you won't have any face left.'

'You – you're a copper! You wouldn't—'

Roger raised his voice so that it sounded clearly in every corner of the big shed; he was afraid that the police might start their raid too soon, that he hadn't left enough time, but his voice did not quiver.

'Listen, all of you,' he said. 'There are fifty policemen outside. They're wearing protective uniforms. If that woman officer falls into the tank, every one of you will be accessories to murder. And Menzies won't be able to help you – *he* won't have any face, any eyes, any lips—'

'Let her go!' screamed Menzies.

'Give yourselves up,' Roger went on in the same clear voice 'First bring her here, then give yourselves up.'

Into the shocked silence, the cherubic man said: 'Give us a chance to go, West – then *she* can go.'

'Send her down to me,' Roger insisted.

'Let her go!' screeched Menzies.

'Hold her there,' the cherubic man said. 'He can burn Menzies up, he can't burn us all.' He drew nearer, a more deadly enemy than Menzies, his nerve much stronger. He leapt to one side, so that Roger could see him only out of the corner of his eye. 'You've got one chance, West. You wouldn't come in here without a radio. Tell your men to let us through. When the last one of us is out, you can go and cut her free. That'll make you a hero, won't it?'

There was a vicious note in his voice, malevolence even more horrible in his expression.

'I'll give you ten seconds,' he said. 'If you haven't sent word by then – in she'll go. *I'll* push her in myself.'

He moved towards the stairs.

'No!' screamed Menzies. 'You'll get us killed, you—'

In a frenzy of fear-given strength he flung himself at the man and carried him headlong to the floor.

Roger heard the thump of their falling and then, gun in hand, moved towards the stairs and the platform and Hilary Reed, and the men on either side of her.

Quite suddenly, the two men turned and ran.

Hilary Reed was quivering from head to foot and yet she managed to smile as Roger pushed the hood further from her face. The ropes which held her to the safety fence were not tight enough to hurt. Roger cut her free, and with infinite care led her along the edge of the platform to safety. By then a dozen police were streaming into the factory, a few of the 'workmen' were showing fight, but most were giving themselves up quietly. Two policemen were at the side of the vat to help Roger and the girl.

The first thing she said as she slipped out of the hood was:

'You're a fine one to tell me not to be a heroine.' But she said it through her tears.

CHAPTER TWENTY-TWO

LARK'S SONG

On the way to the Yard, Hilary talked – of what she had found in the office at Lark's clinic, and what Lark and Delafield had said to her, so sure had they been of their victory. They would eventually have killed her, of course, because of what she knew.

'I don't really know why they didn't do it at once,' she said huskily. 'I think it could have been just in case they needed to do a deal at the last minute.'

'Let's hope it was something a little more humane than that,' Roger said comfortingly, but not believing what he had suggested.

'I'm not sure,' she said. 'I'm really not sure. Delafield seemed to enjoy causing pain. I've come across some sadists but he's by far the worst I've ever met.' She shivered. 'He *is* Young's half-brother by the way – all the intolerance of the one turned to licentiousness in the other. He worked against his half-brother because Young knew what he was doing, and had to be kept silent. Half – more than half – of what happened was to bring people to heel, Mr West.'

Roger said: 'Such as?'

'Clive Davidson, who was the salesman for the organization, wanted more than his share, and threatened to squeal if he didn't get it. So, they worked on him with that poor girl at Chelsea.'

'Is he dead?'

'He was too dangerous to them to live.'

'So he was pushed in.'

'Delafield told me he was, when warning me what would happen when I fell in.'

Roger said quietly: 'No heroine, Miss Reed?'

'There was a time when I positively hated myself,' she said vehemently, but after a pause she went on: 'The Australian Wainwright wanted a bigger cut, and *he* was attacked. I think we'll find he left the Lark Club matches about for us to find – telling us where to look without committing himself with us. Some of the members of the Lark Club knew what was going on and threatened to tell the police – that was why the club was raided. And when I thought Lark was shocked because a member had died, in fact he had just been told I was from the Yard – one of the thieves was there, and saw me. The man was at the plant when you arrived, and took pleasure in telling me how smart he'd been. The little tape-recorder was to pick up any conversation which might threaten danger; all the club-rooms were bugged, sir.'

Roger grimaced. 'We got far too much wrong.'

'You got enough right, sir,' she said, warmly. 'Are you going on to see Lark?'

'Yes.'

'I'd – I'd very much like to come,' Hilary said, and added with a rush: 'And I'm sure Inspector Moriarty would, too.'

They were very near the Yard.

'I think I'll send you home,' he said. 'You've had a worse time than you think. As for Moriarty . . .'

As he told her, he was astonished to see the distress which showed in her expression; the news seemed to shatter her as even her ordeal by suspense had not succeeded in doing.

Lark, so pale, so distinguished and striking looking, so poised, said earnestly:

'Mr West, this is *not* true. I assure you, *I* know nothing about it. Delafield must have been using these premises as a cover, he – I am shocked. *Deeply* shocked. I am indeed. The death of that charming young woman is – too terrible to contemplate. I do assure you—'

'He didn't kill her,' Roger said coldly. 'You haven't a chance, Lark, and there'll be more serious charges. For the moment I am charging you with wilfully obstructing a police officer in the execution of her duty.'

Lark stopped protesting; for a few moments he looked horrified; then he began to talk so fast it was difficult to understand him. He *had* organized the burglaries, he *had* used the club as a blind, he *did* take in professional thieves pretending they were patients, he *had* authorized the acid spraying:

'. . . but never with intent to kill, I swear it! And I knew nothing about the murders, absolutely nothing. I never *went* to the plant, Delafield dealt with Menzies. I swear it.'

It was a long time before he stopped singing his hopeless song.

And that's the long and short of it, sir,' Roger said to Coppell, next morning. 'The clinic and the club were fronts to keep a gang of thieves at the ready, the plant was used whenever big raids were planned. The hard stones and the pure metals didn't suffer from the acid, they could always be picked out of the sludge. The day and evening shifts knew nothing about the night shift, and the main tanks are being cleaned out today. I should say we'll find a couple of million pounds' worth of precious stones there. May I ask a favour?'

Coppell nodded, smiling.

'Can my two sons watch the dredging – young Richard nearly caught some acid in his face, and this—'

'Yes, of course. Meant to tell you before how sorry I was about that,' Coppell said. 'Why attack *him*, Handsome?'

Roger said: 'I'd say it was an attempt to scare me off. Lark and Delafield were afraid I knew more than I did, and they used the terror method – they couldn't imagine anyone being able to withstand the threat of acid. They tried first to discredit me by sending the photograph, and the anonymous letter.'

Coppell nodded. 'And Moriarty?'

Roger said: 'He'll have to be dismissed, I'm afraid.'

'Of course. What about a charge?'

'No need to be vindictive, surely,' Roger said. 'Unless you feel—'

'You tell him he's got to go,' Coppell said. 'I hope he'll live to thank you.'

Moriarty had aged ten years overnight, and he looked as if he were suffering from ague. He stood up from the bed in the cell when Roger appeared, a copy of the *Evening Echo* falling from his lap. He did not speak.

The officer in charge of cells left them together.

Roger said, with an effort: 'It could have been a lot worse, thank God. Your career in the Force is over, but if you go into private security and can use your head, you won't waste all you've learned.' Moriarty's lips were working. 'Miss Reed sends her regards,' Roger added – and broke off.

157

The next few minutes were among the worst he had ever known, for he hated to see a man break down and cry as if his heart would break.

Roger and his two sons, the Superintendent in charge of the Laboratory, several experts from Hatton Garden, and Detective Constable Hilary Reed were present when the sludge at the bottom of the vat was washed, and rewashed, and washed yet again, until the diamonds began to shine and sparkle.

Diamond after diamond, jewel after jewel was found. Here and there were gaps in the setting where the pearls had been, but that was all.

'Marvellous!' exclaimed Richard. 'You wouldn't think stuff which could make such a mess of your face would *clean* anything, would you?' He looked ingenuously into Hilary Reed's eyes. 'If you're not on duty, do you think I could have a ride – or even a *drive* – in your car? It's a wow.'

'You're a—' began Martin.

'Would you like to, as well?' Hilary asked him.

Martin's eyes lit up, 'You mean, we *may*?'

'After what I owe your father, that's nothing at all,' Hilary assured him.

Roger, overhearing, moved across and said:

'When you've finished your good deed with my sons, Constable, will you do another?' Her eyes questioned him. 'Go and see how Moriarty's taking it,' Roger said, and added quietly: 'He needs a shoulder to lean on.'

'I don't know whether you two realize it,' Hilary Reed said to Martin and Richard, both glowing from their drive, 'but your father is the kindest man alive.'

'Wish he'd prove it to us, sometimes,' Martin sighed.

But he winked.

158

BIOGRAPHICAL NOTES ON JOHN CREASEY

One of the major factors in John Creasey's ever increasing popularity is undoubtedly his talent for viewing and so portraying his characters as living beings: each with his own special problem, each with his own hopes and dreams and fears. John Creasey has now written nearly 500 books, and in essence this extraordinary achievement is a testament to his penetrating observation and understanding of human behaviour. Criminals, their victims, the police – all he writes of are touched with this very real compassion.

He has long been noted for his use of sociological and industrial backgrounds (*A Gun For Inspector West* – 1953, and *Death In Cold Print* – 1961, are typical examples), portraying each with meticulous accuracy while demonstrating how the life of any man, in any walk of life, may be affected by the activities of criminals hitherto unknown to him. As his researches deepened his lifelong interest in social and political affairs, he soon turned part of his great energy to campaigning for National Savings, United Europe (1945–50), Road Safety, Oxfam, and other national and local causes. Simultaneously, he took a close interest in politics, serving the Liberal Party with characteristic enthusiasm for over thirty years.

Despite all this, he has still found time to travel very widely and that innate power of observation – and a strong streak of idealism – quickened his interest in world poverty and world problems. The more he saw, the more he became aware of the interdependence of people everywhere – and the more convinced he became that failure to recognize this interdependence was the cause of most of the social, economic, and political evils of the world.

(This theme – that it is Mankind's destiny to work together for the common good – has indeed been a feature of two of his finest series: the 'police procedural' *Gideons* and the later *Wests*.)

It was a natural step for him to apply his beliefs to the British scene. And almost single-handed, he started a political movement – All Party Alliance – the purpose of which is to get the best men from all the parties working together in government. It is characteristic of Creasey that he spends very large proportion of his income on this movement, beside publishing* a monthly journal – *APA News* – in an effort spread the ideas in which he believes and by which he worl and lives.

*From 19 Coton Road, Nuneaton, Warwicks.